Dear Reader,

As a diehard introvert, I've always wished for a body double to take my place in socially challenging situations. Technology and Mother Nature, however, continue to deny me. The most I can do is put on a happy face and plow through it without incurring hexes or starting feuds. Frankly, I think that's what most of us do. We put on a specific "face" and act accordingly: a competent face; an authoritative face; a lover's face; a road-rage face (although my sunglasses usually cover up this last one).

My character Valerie simply takes this coping mechanism to an enjoyable extreme. I've loved working with Valerie. She's such a complex character—irreverent and so savvy. And I envy her the joys of her carefree vampy side. She has such fun driving Jack crazy with it. I hope you enjoy their story as much as I loved writing it.

Best,

Natalie Stenzel

P.S.—I love to hear from readers! Drop by my Web site at www.NatalieStenzel.com or snail mail me at P.O. Box 182, Midlothian, VA 23113.

"It appears being locked in the basement won't be so bad after all."

Jack emerged from the wine cellar holding a bottle and corkscrew. "So, we've got all night to talk. Can I pick the first topic?"

Valerie sighed. After falling down the stairs, then being locked up with a gorgeous, but thoroughly frustrating man, alcohol—not conversation—was the first order of business. "Not until after I've had some of that wine."

Just as he extended his hand to offer the freshly opened bottle, he frowned and pulled it back.

"What?" She scowled at him. "If anyone around here needs a drink, I'd think it would be me. I did just take a header, remember?"

"Exactly. I wonder if we should be careful, in case of concussion or something."

"I appreciate the concern, Jack, but I'm okay. I think we would have gotten a clue by now if anything were seriously wrong with me."

"I don't know, Val. We better not take any chances."

"Let's put this a different way, then. Hand over the bottle and no one gets hurt."

Seeking Miss Scarlet

Natalie Stenzel

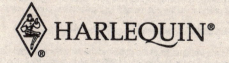

TORONTO • NEW YORK • LONDON
AMSTERDAM • PARIS • SYDNEY • HAMBURG
STOCKHOLM • ATHENS • TOKYO • MILAN • MADRID
PRAGUE • WARSAW • BUDAPEST • AUCKLAND

If you purchased this book without a cover you should be aware that this book is stolen property. It was reported as "unsold and destroyed" to the publisher, and neither the author nor the publisher has received any payment for this "stripped book."

ISBN 0-373-44212-2

SEEKING MISS SCARLET

Copyright © 2005 by Natale Nogosek Stenzel.

All rights reserved. Except for use in any review, the reproduction or utilization of this work in whole or in part in any form by any electronic, mechanical or other means, now known or hereafter invented, including xerography, photocopying and recording, or in any information storage or retrieval system, is forbidden without the written permission of the publisher, Harlequin Enterprises Limited, 225 Duncan Mill Road, Don Mills, Ontario, Canada M3B 3K9.

All characters in this book have no existence outside the imagination of the author and have no relation whatsoever to anyone bearing the same name or names. They are not even distantly inspired by any individual known or unknown to the author, and all incidents are pure invention.

This edition published by arrangement with Harlequin Books S.A.

® and TM are trademarks of the publisher. Trademarks indicated with ® are registered in the United States Patent and Trademark Office, the Canadian Trade Marks Office and in other countries.

www.eHarlequin.com

Printed in U.S.A.

ABOUT THE AUTHOR

Natalie Stenzel was a girl who just couldn't keep her nose out of (gasp!) a romance novel. Still, she denied her dreamy inclinations long enough to earn respectable degrees in English literature and magazine journalism from the University of Missouri-Columbia. She even flirted with business writing and freelancing for a while, and considered going back to school for another respectable degree...only to return to her one true love: romance. Born and raised in St. Louis, Missouri, Natalie now resides in lovely Virginia with her husband and two children, happy to live a dream (or several) come true.

Books by Natalie Stenzel

HARLEQUIN FLIPSIDE
 4—FORGET PRINCE CHARMING
12—POP-UP DATING
24—ALL SHOOK UP

Don't miss any of our special offers. Write to us at the following address for information on our newest releases.

Harlequin Reader Service
U.S.: 3010 Walden Ave., P.O. Box 1325, Buffalo, NY 14269
Canadian: P.O. Box 609, Fort Erie, Ont. L2A 5X3

To Steve, who should hereafter consider himself a given in every book dedication. You're my rock and my inspiration.

Special thanks also to Carolyn Greene, a wonderful writer, an enlightened teacher and a supportive friend. Thank you!

1

"OH, MY GOD, she's already dead."

To the oohs and aahs of surrounding bystanders, Jack Harrison dropped to his knees, his heart pounding a vicious beat as he stared at the prone woman.

On the polished wooden floor of the burgundy salon lay Valerie Longstreet, her body as still as death. A grisly red stain, thick and shiny and fresh, surrounded an obscene little hole in the bodice of her gold sequined dress.

Sequined...? He frowned. Sure, Valerie had a taste for glamour, but *sequins?* Usually, she wore high-quality silk or snappy little suits paired with stiletto heels. She'd even go so far as to wear a smart fedora tilted seductively low over one eye, just to make a statement. But never sequins.

And her face...she looked different, with her eyelids darkened and lined to dramatic effect. A mole she didn't have was inked into a provocative spot near the corner of her mouth.

The mouth tightened briefly.

"Valerie?" His voice sounded faint to his own ears.

Her eyes slitted open, and if he wasn't mistaken, that was a glare he saw in their usually warm depths. After studying her for a baffled moment, he glanced up, finally noticing the elaborate layout of the room. A crystal decanter and two half-filled brandy glasses, the eerie glow cast by the restless flames of a candelabra, heavy drapes billowing out from an open window. At any moment, he expected the silence of the room to be rent by a wild clap of thunder, a shouted accusation—

At a soft noise behind him, Jack pivoted. He saw a blur of black and white...a lacy maid's apron over black skirts...tuxedos and silver trays...and familiar faces betraying mild alarm. And then he focused on a group of elegantly dressed strangers, about a dozen of them, all staring expectantly at him. Not horrified, but rather intrigued. Excited even.

Valerie's guests.

Jack closed his eyes, enjoying the pleasant aftermath of making an ass of himself. As gracefully as he was able—considering he'd looked briefly into the jaws of death, only to discover it was all child's play—he rose to his feet and backed away from the "body."

"Jack." An older woman glided toward him. Valerie's aunt Lillian, he remembered. The writer. She wore her usual floaty silks with a fake mink stole draped carefully around her shoulders. "You decided to join us. That's *wonderful*."

She glanced around, an expectant gleam in her eyes. "Ladies and gentlemen, we have a treat for you tonight. Not only do we have a murder mystery for you to solve, but we also have an expert in our midst." She smiled coyly at him.

"Allow me to introduce our neighbor, Jack Harrison. He spent eight years with the Chicago Police Department and now runs his very own detective agency. His office is just down the street from us here at the Longstreet Inn and Mystery Theater." She winked confidingly at her audience. "Maybe with a little encouragement we can persuade him to aid our investigations."

Under her breath, she murmured to him, "Just consider it public relations. Maybe you'll get a plug in the society rags."

A polite round of murmurs and smiles followed, while Jack worked to contain his chaotic emotions. As the murmurs rose to excited chattering and the occasional loudly expressed opinion, he glanced down to where Valerie still lay on the hard floor.

She had shifted position slightly, he noticed, his sense of humor taking up where horror had left off. Still gazing at Val's artificially pale face, he reluctantly spoke up. "Sure. I'd be happy to help."

Bright red lips, shocking and full against heavily powdered skin, twitched and then tilted just a little. Upward. Until the corpse wore a faint but very pleased...smirk.

"SO WHAT TRAGEDY or act of God brought the good detective to our performance tonight?"

Valerie glanced up at the amused question. "Who, Jack? I have no idea."

Lillian nodded silently. They both stood just outside the door to the Longstreet Inn's library, an inspiring choice of "war room" for the amateur sleuths' heated discussions.

After they retired from the war room, guests might go upstairs to relax in the inn's homey guest rooms. Or, if they declined the Longstreet Inn's excellent postmystery drinks and dessert, they might go out on the town to enjoy nearby restaurants or boutiques.

Any number of quaint shops, bars and eateries lined the streets of Soulard, an eclectic and historic neighborhood of red brick row houses in south St. Louis. Longstreet Inn and

Mystery Theater occupied a building and corner lot that once comprised one of the larger residences in the area.

But the night was still young and guests of the inn still had some sleuthing to do—perhaps another hour's worth, Valerie surmised, depending on Jack's input. Assuming he was still willing to help. He'd acted so weird earlier.

"I didn't even hear him come in, and then there he was, leaning over me." Valerie shrugged, feeling the sticky red goo tug at the flesh beneath her dress. It itched. She should have worn a slip, but she hadn't been able to find one at the last minute and time had run short on her.

Simone better have a very good reason for calling in sick, Valerie thought grimly. She'd only hired the actress six months ago and was less than pleased with the woman's job performance. Or lack of it. Simone had found one reason or another to opt out of half of the shows so far. Eye-catchingly beautiful, possibly talented and completely unreliable. Valerie was convinced that artistic temperaments would eventually put an end to her sanity. Or at least her business.

"Yes, wasn't that strange?" Lillian tipped her glasses to peer into the room at Jack and their guests. "Why tonight of all nights? Jack's never attended a performance before."

"God knows I've invited him enough. Stubborn man."

Lillian smiled. "Maybe you wore him down."

"I doubt it." Valerie folded her arms across her *wounded* chest and studied the man's back. "You know what's strange, though? I got the distinct impression that he really thought I was dead. Either that or he was putting on a damn good show for my guests." She raised an eyebrow. "In which case, I should probably hire him for his acting talents alone."

Lillian chuckled. "You might have to. He's a popular man this evening."

Their guests, a group united in obsession over Agatha Christie and the great Sherlock Holmes, enjoyed a companion fascination for real private detectives. They had already transferred their hero worship to the handsome investigator in their midst, and were now bombarding him with theories and questions intended to illustrate their own deductive skills. Jack, to give him his due, patiently addressed each query as best he could.

Valerie grinned. In fact, Jack was doing exactly what she'd begged him to do ever since he opened his agency just down the street from her. A conjunction of their businesses had just seemed logical to her—logical and *profitable*.

"Well, ladies and gentlemen, it looks like you have this case under control. I think I'll leave it in your capable hands while I discuss a few matters with your hostess." Jack smiled charmingly. With a farewell nod he exited the library and closed the door behind him.

When he turned to face the two women, the smile was a distant memory. No big surprise, really. The man rarely gave up a full-blown smile.

"Hello, Jack." Val flashed him a dazzler of a grin. Sure, it was intended to provoke. Jack was fun to provoke. Mild annoyance never looked sexier on a guy than it did on Jack. She resisted a sigh. "You were just wonderful in there with my guests. I think you're truly gifted."

"Wonderful. Don't get any ideas." He opened his mouth as though to pursue the subject further, then closed it with an air of distraction. "I didn't think you acted in the mysteries."

"I usually don't, but we needed someone to fill in at the

last minute, and I fit the costume. Reasonably." She braced her hands on her hips and inhaled deeply, expanding her chest upward to ease the binding around her rib cage. Stupid dress had been suffocating her all evening. She looked up and caught him staring, eyebrows raised, at her generously bared chest-level.

When his eyes glazed over, she bit back a chuckle and flashed him another dazzling smile. "Like the dress? It's borrowed."

"Huh?" The gaze, reluctantly, rose to meet hers. "Oh. It didn't look like your usual..." He scowled, the glazed look fading as he refocused. "Forget the dress. You and I need to get a few things straight. Sure, I cooperated tonight, but that was strictly a one-time deal. So you can save your strategies and fiction for your guests. They're wasted on me."

"My strategies and my fiction? You're losing me, Jack."

"I'm saying, damn it, that I will *not* be your trained monkey." He scowled. "No matter how hard you try to sell it."

"Well all you have to do is say so. Sure, I've tried to talk you into participating in our productions, but I certainly didn't think I was giving you a *hard* sell."

"Oh, no? Why the note, then?" Jack sounded slightly harassed. "If that's not a hard sell, I don't know what is. Whether it was for the consulting job you've been trying to ram down my throat or for more personal reasons—" He shook his head, obviously disgusted. "Damn it, Val, I thought you had more class than that."

"And from here we degenerate into argument." Lillian spoke over him. "So I'll just leave you two alone to get it out of your systems while I tend to our guests."

"Hmm? Oh, thanks, Lillian." Val gave her a distracted nod. Lillian slipped into the war room and shut the door.

Val turned back to Jack. "So I've been tacky, hmm? Suppose you try explaining this one more time, but *without* the monkeys and the dammits. Just what are you accusing me of?"

"This." He held up a parchment-colored envelope. "I found it under my door this afternoon."

She glanced at it with only mild curiosity before its significance registered. "Oh. A *note* note. Someone sent you one, too? Like the kind I've been getting? The goofy stalker threats?"

"Don't give me this 'someone' crap. *You* slid it under my door in some juvenile ploy to get me out here." He looked honestly baffled. "Geez, Val. Aren't there easier ways to get a guy's attention?"

"Excuse me?" She raised her nose in mock hauteur. "Do I *look* like I need to use stupid ploys to attract a man?"

"*No.* That's what's throwing me off."

"Oh. Well, thank you. I think." No, huh? Interesting. Tabling the note discussion in favor of one dearer to her heart and libido, she eyed him appraisingly. "So tell me, then. What exactly *would* it take to get you to go out with me?"

"You could try *asking.*"

"Really?" She smiled and lowered her lashes for seductive punch. It was a good look for her, she knew. One of the few expressions she'd truly perfected for the small screen. Tearful angst hadn't worked for her—but sexy smiles she could do. "Okay. Jack Harrison, will you go out with me?"

"*No.*"

"No?" She blinked at his vehemence. He hadn't even *hesitated*. But *he* was the one who suggested— "Well, why not?"

"Lots of reasons, but I'm thinking it's mostly your psycho potential." His eyebrows lowered. "What kind of woman sends threatening notes just to get a guy's attention?"

"I didn't send you the note."

"Well, somebody did."

She rolled her eyes. "So naturally it had to be me, right? Good grief. Let me see this note. What, is somebody threatening to do you in? Smash your magnifying glass? Burn all your pleated khakis?" *Jeans.* For purely salacious reasons, she'd love to see the man in jeans for a change.

Looking truly harassed now, Jack handed her the opened envelope. A familiar little crease marred the top of it, just above the seal.

Plucking it out of his fingers, Valerie opened it to find something different than the sender's usual collage-inspired message comprised of cutout magazine and newsprint words. This time the envelope contained a printed invitation to a funeral.

In memory of the late Valerie Longstreet.

Mildly taken aback, Val stared at it for a moment. "So I'm still the one getting knocked off."

"Sure you are." He threw her a derisive look.

"Oh, come on. I swear I didn't have anything to do with this note. I didn't plan it, I didn't write it, I didn't have it printed up and I didn't send it to you. It's not my style." Valerie gave the note a contemptuous little flick with her nail. "I mean, talk about lame." She continued in a mockingly macabre tone. "'You're invited to a funeral for the late Valerie Longstreet, at a place and time to be determined.' What, like when my *dead body* shows up? What kind of stupidity is that? Not to mention lazy. Any decent stalker would at least glance at the calendar and take a whack at a real date."

Jack was shaking his head, his expression still watchful. "No, a date would amount to a commitment. This leaves things conveniently open-ended. So now, as a man of ethics, I understand I'm supposed to ride off to your 'rescue'?"

Mostly fed up now, Val folded her arms and met his eyes squarely. "Obviously you doubt my ethics, so let's try for logic and efficiency, shall we? Think about it. If I were so utterly desperate for your body—not to mention underhanded and completely devoid of flair—I'd just show up at your door naked." She gestured with casual confidence. "Nine out of ten guys would simply take me up on my offer."

"True enough. Except it's not just my *body* you're after."

"No, darling. It's your *mind*, your *wit*, your sense of *humor*. You slay me with your charm and easy smiles." Valerie lowered her lashes in a flirtatious display that was entirely disingenuous.

She watched the tiny quirk of his lips. Exactly what she was going for. It meant she was finally getting through to him. She had more class than to use fake threats to snare a guy's attention. Aside from their current disagreement, however, she generally moved heaven and earth to invite those little lip curls and quirks of his. Not only did they kick up a sexy dent in his right cheek, but seeing one of them was like scoring a hard-won point against the man's romantic defenses.

And the man had some damn imposing defenses. Calling Jack "reserved" didn't do the situation justice.

Over the past weeks, she'd come to realize, though, that Jack wasn't as solemn and negative as he pretended. No, he had a sense of humor, if a dark one, and she had yet to see him truly smile at her, but those infrequent little lip twitches of his were dead giveaways from an otherwise mysterious man.

So it was a subtle, sexy game they played—at least in her mind. He tried his damnedest not to give anything away, and she gave her all trying to break through despite his reserve. He wasn't as immune to her as he'd like her to think.

"Seriously, Val. You and I both know you have other motives for directing a note like that to me. Besides your unexplainable infatuation—"

"Gee, is this my cue to swoon or to blush?" She widened her eyes like the dizziest of ditzes, and watched his eyes glint in reluctant amusement. *Byplay.* They had terrific byplay. That was the attraction for her, and—she'd swear—for him, too.

"—you've also been nagging me to cooperate with you professionally."

"Well, that's true enough." She met his gaze unflinchingly. "It could be lucrative for both of us. Think about it, Jack. A licensed detective and a mystery dinner theater…it just begs for conjunctive business efforts. You could be my consultant, doing just what you did tonight with my guests. Helping them with their cases. I'd include you in my advertising, which would gain you free publicity and even a modest, supplementary income from me—"

"And it would do worlds of good for *your* bottom line."

"Naturally." She smiled. "It's all win-win for both of us."

"So you did send the note."

"*No.* Sheesh. Who's nagging whom around here? *I didn't send the stupid note.* I don't operate that way. Honestly, Jack, when have I ever been anything but shamelessly up-front with you?"

He pondered for a moment, then shoved his hands in his

pockets with a sigh. "I'll give you that much. You're nothing if not shameless *and* up-front. Maybe you didn't do it."

"Gosh, you're perceptive." She marveled facetiously. "Must be that P.I. training."

He ignored her comment. "Who did send it, then?"

"One of Lillian's writing students? Your secret admirer? The mailman? One of our ghosts?" She shrugged carelessly. "Who knows. Who *cares?* The more attention you pay a wacko, the more legitimacy you lend him."

"Sort of like your ghosts?" He raised an eyebrow.

"Hey, don't knock 'em. No mystery dinner theater is complete without a ghost, and we have *three* of the genuine article." They were a promotional gold mine, in fact.

"Three. Wow." He gave her a deadpan look. "Then it's amazing that I've never run into one of them."

"Really, Jack. Ghosts don't just jump up and say hello. There's no mystique in that." She waved a hand carelessly. "You'd have to live here to understand how it is."

"Guess I'll just have to take your word for it, then."

"Gee, *that'd* be a nice change."

The door to the war room opened and Lillian emerged with a speculative smile. "Ah. You're speaking and no one's bleeding. *Wonderful.*" She carefully closed the door.

Jack gave her a rueful smile.

Lillian rated a smile? How was that fair, damn it?

"So would it be too *incendiary* to ask what brought all of this on?" Lillian asked Jack.

Val answered for him. "Someone slid a note under his door. Much like the silly threats I've been getting."

"*No.*"

Jack handed Lillian the preprinted card. She read it quickly and gasped. "*Val.* You saw?"

"Yes, I saw. And Jack thinks—or thought—that *I* sent it to him."

"You?" Lillian paused. "That would be a fun plot twist, I suppose, but not at all your style, darling."

"That's what I said—over and over. I think I finally got it through his thick skull."

"Well, good." Lillian turned a stern look on Jack. "So what are you going to do about this?"

"Nothing."

"*Nothing?*" Lillian looked outraged. "But this is virtually a death threat. Against a defenseless young lady. Why, any detective worth his training would rise up to defend her."

Val cringed inwardly. God, she didn't need him guilted or obligated into taking action on her behalf. Talk about smothering any potential for romance. "Aunt Lillian—"

"*I* think you should move in and act as her bodyguard—whether she wants you to or not." Her eyes growing dewy with drama, Lillian continued without pause. "Isn't that what an *honorable* man would do? One who's been trained to protect the innocent and uphold the law?"

"Well…yes." Jack seemed uncomfortable, obviously torn between battling what he perceived as the ridiculous and not contradicting a woman who was his elder while she prodded at his honor.

Val shoved aside her own discomfort to consider new possibilities. Her aunt had definitely found a chink in the man's armor. So to speak. No, Val hadn't sent the note and *wouldn't*. Her moral fiber was woven a little more tightly than that, thank you very much. But…since the note, after all, was right there and not a product of her own manipulations…

"You know, Aunt Lillian may have a point." Val spoke slowly, then at Jack's appalled expression, she smiled. "No, not about the guilt trip and honor and all that. I mean about the value of precautionary measures. Sure, I have a hard time believing these notes are anything more than a prank, but I suppose it couldn't hurt to play it safe. Especially if those precautionary measures served other, more profitable aims. Right?"

Jack groaned. "Give it up, Val."

"Seriously. You could be my bodyguard—and you'd even have a built-in, legitimate cover for hanging around here so much. We wouldn't, after all, want to advertise the fact that I, and now you, have been receiving notes like this. There might be bottom-line repercussions if we did. No, you could just say you were acting as a consultant while you secretly protected my body." She grinned at him. "You'd have guaranteed income for a couple of easy—possibly enjoyable—jobs. You couldn't lose."

He gave her a knowing look. "You have a one-track mind."

"A couple of tracks, actually, but business is my passion."

"Yeah, I'll buy that." There was an edge to his voice.

"So what do you say? Want to be my business-consultant-slash-bodyguard? I can't afford to pay you a mint, but surely we could negotiate something to satisfy us both." She chuckled wickedly. "Honestly, that was *not* a proposition. I swear."

He just shook his head, but Valerie was almost certain he'd cracked another smile under that scowl he worked so hard to maintain. She was getting good at this.

"I'm flattered by the offer. But I'll have to pass on it."

"Oh, but Jack—" Lillian's voice rose in protest.

He shifted his attention to the older woman, his manner patient—certainly more patient than he was with Val.

"Lillian, I understand you're worried about your niece, but I honestly think this is all smoke. She's *fine*. She'll *be* fine. She's a smart woman who can take care of herself."

"No bodyguard?" Lillian sounded disappointed.

"It's not necessary."

"Oh, Jack." Valerie gave him a wounded look, eyes wide and faintly mocking. "You'd go off and leave me alone? *Defenseless?*"

Jack eyed her shrewdly and she *knew* that was a smile. It was there, a small one, but she could see it. "Valerie, I don't think there's a defenseless bone in that body of yours."

Valerie laughed outright, relaxing the deliberately vampy stance she'd affected earlier. "Okay, okay. In the interest of good neighborly relations, I'll give the soft sell—and hard sell, though I swear I don't *do* hard sells—a rest."

"Thank God."

"So. Just so we understand each other..."

Jack wearily closed his eyes and Val bit back a laugh.

She forced a casual tone. "You never *once* thought I was in danger. Right? You got this note and immediately assumed *I* was the one who sent it." She eyed him closely.

He nodded with exaggerated patience.

Satisfied, she lowered her lashes and spoke in a soft, provoking little voice. "So tell me then, Jack. What was that little drama you enacted while I was laid out dead on the floor?" She let her lips curve, just the tiniest bit. "Admit it. For just a moment in there, you thought someone had really shot me." And it had bothered him. An awful lot.

He glanced away, shoving his hands in the pockets of those khaki pants he always wore. Thick, almost black wavy hair skimmed the collar of his green polo shirt. For some time now, she'd wanted to rake her nails through the silky strands and ruffle it free of its tidy simplicity. Maybe rock his orderly world a little. He was so controlled. Usually.

He hadn't been controlled in the least when he'd dropped to his knees beside her while she lay on the floor. Probably the most hopeful sign yet. He cared. He was attracted *and* he cared.

He looked back at her now, his hazel eyes opaque. "What can I say? Temporary insanity? Reason deserted me. Sorry for the display in front of your guests." He shrugged casually and shifted his gaze to a point beyond her shoulder. "You make a convincing corpse when you set your mind to it."

"A convincing corpse?" Valerie cocked her head and turned to Lillian. "I think I've just been insulted. Or complimented." She blinked in mock confusion. "I'm at a loss."

Lillian gazed fondly at her. "Well, you do have a way with makeup, dear. In fact, you still look like death warmed over."

Valerie touched a finger to the blue-tinged hollow of her cheek and smiled proudly. "I do my best."

Jack groaned. "You're both nuts. I'm out of here."

As he strode for the door, Val called after him in a mocking singsong. "Don't be a stranger."

The door closed behind him.

Val and Lillian exhaled softly and exchanged a glance.

"He's *so* hot." Val fanned herself.

"Obscenely attractive," Lillian agreed. "Why, his eyes positively *glittered* with suspicion. I thought I would swoon."

"Oh, I *know*." Val giggled then gave her aunt a sly look. "So tell me the truth. Did *you* send him the note?"

"And threaten my own niece?"

Val snorted. "Your ghoulish reputation precedes you."

Lillian waved a hand carelessly. "But, darling, what an obvious ploy. Would I be so foolish?"

Val considered. "Maybe not. I wonder who sent it then."

"I'm betting on the ghosts." Lillian spoke slowly, her eyes speculative.

Val laughed. "Oh, please. You think it's the *bride*, maybe?"

Lillian frowned. "No. She's harmless. Conflicted but harmless. The other two, though, they're tougher to figure out. Such restless spirits."

Ghostly stalkers. Right. "Lillian, I love you, but you're losing it. Maybe you need a vacation from all the blood and gore you write."

"Nevertheless." She plucked the note card out of Valerie's hand. "I'll take this." Carefully, still holding the corner only, Lillian marched toward the stairs, silky skirts flowing and mink stole swaying gently to and fro. "*Evidence*, you know."

"Definitely in need of a vacation." Val pondered. "Or…a man, maybe? There's a thought."

"I heard that, Valerie Longstreet." Lillian's voice floated down to her.

"Heard what?" Val approached the bottom of the stairs, glanced around to see no guests were within earshot, then grinned up at her aunt. "That I said you needed to get laid?"

Eyes sparkling with humor, Lillian tut-tutted. "That's my darling Valerie. Talented actress, budding entrepreneur and, amazingly, a full-blown *chauvinist*. I'm *so* proud."

2

"How much? Never mind. Thanks for your time." Hanging up the phone in disgust, Val crossed through another entry in the phone book. "That's highway robbery. Which is downright ironic, if you think about it. Security experts taking clients for a long, expensive ride? It's criminal."

"Oh, there you are." Lillian strolled into Val's office. "I was looking for you earlier."

"Well, you found me." Val stared at the phone book and circled a larger ad. Bigger ads meant more income meant more success meant greater competence…? Either that or more highway robbery. "Any chance you also found my coffee mug?"

"The new one?" Lillian grimaced in sympathy. "*Blue* glass."

Val sighed. "That's the one. And my blue fountain pen's still missing, so I was hoping I'd just misplaced the mug."

"That's possible, I suppose." Lillian sounded kind but doubting.

"No, you don't." Val frowned absently. "The bride strikes again. You know, normal people don't have to worry about kleptomaniac ghosts."

Lillian chuckled. "Eleanor's not a thief. She's just indecisive. She'll figure things out eventually."

"No, she won't. She couldn't make a decision when she was alive, so why start now?"

"True enough. Oh, well. Be patient. The mug and pen will turn up eventually. All the other stuff has." Dismissing an old subject, Lillian spared a glance over Val's shoulder. "Ah. Security. You're finally going to update our system?"

"In theory." She glanced up. "So you were looking for me?"

"Oh, yes. But that was earlier. Nothing urgent." She spread her stack of magazines on a table next to Valerie's desk, then sat with a graceful scooping of her skirts. "I wanted to discuss some ideas with you, but have since decided to let them cook a little first." She set her scissors on the table and perched half-moon glasses on her nose. "You were gone such a long time this morning I was afraid you'd gotten caught in traffic downtown, with that TV program filming and blocking streets."

"No, I actually walked to— Oh, wait!" Val grinned at her aunt. "I forgot to tell you. I ran into Phyllis Burlington today. That's what took me so long. I stopped to talk to her. You know. *The* Phyllis Burlington who reviews restaurants and hotels for *Gateway*?"

"You mean the Phyllis Burlington who writes a trashy gossip column *disguised* as a review column?" Brandishing her little scissors, Lillian scowled as she flipped open a magazine.

"That's the one." Val beamed. "She said she might drop by sometime and review Longstreet Inn and Mystery Theater."

Lillian shook her head. "I wouldn't get my hopes up."

"I know, I know. But this time, we've got that great

write-up in the *SouthCity Journal* to back us up, a brand-new gourmet cook, plus the theater, of course, which is always a novelty. *And*—" Valerie smiled evilly "—I think it's just possible that I *outapathied* her into giving us a review. I was annoyingly blasé this morning. Her type just adores blasé."

"Hmm. I guess I could see that working." Lillian nodded thoughtfully. "How about that? A visit from a vile reviewer. Certainly beats food poisoning and visits from the health department. You know, I still wish you had let me handle that nasty situation. We could have incorporated food poisoning into the story line and just called it a touch of *realism*." Lillian's eyes twinkled with mischief.

"Sure, that would've worked. Although it's a little hard for guests to solve a mystery when they're in the hospital puking their guts up."

"Now, Val, only one guest ended up in the hospital. And it served him right, too, for making such a pig of himself. The others were just a tiny bit nauseous."

Val raised an eyebrow at the understatement but let it pass. "I'm just glad it's behind us and we have a brand-new, seriously hygiene-conscious chef." Val dismissed the subject and turned back to the business at hand. "Ever notice there are a lot of security companies in the phone book?"

"Can't say that I have, actually. Any luck?"

"Nope. But I'm not through yet." Val ran a finger down the column, then stabbed another phone number into the receiver, waiting while it rang. And rang. And rang. "Gee, that's professional. I didn't even get a machine." She hung up.

"Honestly, Valerie. Why don't you just call Jack? I bet he'd recommend someone for you."

"*Oh*, no. I'm avoiding Jack, at least for a few days. If I contact him now, he'll think it's another ploy. Because, apparently, I'm *desperate*." She widened her eyes for effect.

"Oh, I don't think so. This is, after all, a legitimate business inquiry. Security's something detectives and policemen know. At least, better than we do. If you want to update our system here, you should call him and ask for recommendations."

Valerie considered. Her aunt had a point. And Val didn't want to overpay or hire an incompetent. "What if *you* called Jack. And got some names for me." She smiled. "Yes, that's perfect. If you make the call and talk to him—involving *me* not at *all*—then he won't think I'm just making up excuses to talk to him." So *what* if she was being juvenile. Hell, he thought she was sending fake threats just to get his attention. What was that if not juvenile? So she would be juvenile.

Lillian thought for a moment, then smiled brightly. "Excellent idea." She held her hand out for the phone.

Val plugged in the number and handed the receiver to her aunt. She watched expectantly, wishing she could hear his voice.

That was pathetic infatuation for you. Seriously juvenile.

"Hello, Jack?" Lillian spoke pleasantly. "Yes. It's Lillian. Your neighbor at Longstreet Inn. No, Val's fine."

Val raised her eyebrows. *He'd* asked about *her*?

"N-no." Lillian lowered her voice. "She's not in therapy."

Ah. Val closed her eyes, shook her head.

"Yes, well, I was calling to see if you could drop by and help us out with something."

Drop by? Val's eyes opened wide and her head-shaking grew vigorous. "No—"

"Yes, that would be fine. Thank you." She hung up the phone and gazed innocently at her niece.

Val covered her face and mumbled through her fingers. "You're incorrigible."

"Well, really, Val. I think he should take a look at the system we already have before he gives us names, don't you? He might have some expert advice for you."

"Right. Maybe he's dropping by to recommend a good therapist. Someone specializing in fatal-attraction types."

"Now, Val. I'm sure he was just joking about the therapy question."

"Well, *I'm* not. He thinks I'm psycho."

Lillian just patted her hand and chuckled.

With a sigh, Val set aside her discomfort and turned back to her planner. Inquire about security. Check. She skimmed a finger down to the next item on her to-do list and pulled out the schedules for next week.

Scanning the list on autopilot, Val continued to ponder. Lillian had a point about letting Jack see their existing system. She needed to get it updated, and she'd worked too hard to scrape the extra cash together to screw the job up by hiring the wrong people.

"Val, do you suppose insurance would pay for the security system?" Lillian gazed at her over her glasses.

Val paused. "There's a thought. You're brilliant, Lillian. I don't suppose you have the number…? Never mind." She flipped through the phone book until she found insurance agents.

It would be excellent if insurance would pay for this. God knows a little nudge the wrong way in her ledgers could send the inn reeling into bankruptcy. And she couldn't let that happen.

She loved Longstreet Inn and Mystery Theater. It was the vehicle for all her professional dreams, and it allowed her to keep and maintain her grandmother's legacy. This big old house was the most stable home Valerie had ever known. Her parents had died in a car wreck when she was twelve, and her grandmother had taken her in and raised her through those difficult teen years until Val left for college.

She'd been taking acting classes in California and working in a small but prized television role, when she'd learned of her grandmother's death. For Val, that telephone call had marked the end of one life and the beginning of a new one. Sort of a maturing period that lasted mere moments. As for college...Val had left it and dreams of acting behind her and with no regrets. Wonderings, possibly, but no regrets.

And now she had the inn with its lovely mystery performances, and the pseudofamily she'd created with her temperamental artsy types. Lillian, her mother's sister, lived with her now, providing loving companionship, as well as a profitable—*enjoyable*—business partnership.

Together, they'd dreamed up the whole idea of Longstreet Inn and Mystery Theater, offering not just a little bed-and-breakfast, but a gourmet restaurant, elegant but comfortable guest rooms and the novelty of a mystery dinner theater. They offered weekend shows, two weekday dinner shows and Tuesday afternoon matinee performances. With a regular cast of actors, Lillian as in-house mystery writer and Val handling business matters, they managed to change the shows regularly. Eventually, Val wanted to offer a monthly, weeklong mystery package.

Dreams, lots of dreams.

Speaking of dreams—fantasies really, or possibly, humiliating nightmares—Val opened her eyes and gazed fatalistically at her aunt. "So when's Jack coming over?"

"Hmm?" Lillian looked up. She'd gone back to the trade journal she'd been thumbing earlier, a pair of tiny, blue-handled scissors at the ready. Lillian believed in clipping and saving anything that might come in handy for a future whodunit.

"Jack? Is coming when?"

"Oh, any minute now. He said he was on his way out the door, anyway, so sooner was better than later. Wait—" Lillian just held up a finger for silence. A knock sounded at the front door.

Val frowned. "Who knocks on the door of an inn? Just walk in—" Her eyes widened. Of course. Jack would knock.

Lillian turned, a satisfied expression on her face. "That's probably him now. My, but that man is prompt. An admirable quality and all too rare these days. You know, he'd really make a wonderful lover for you."

Valerie choked a little. "Punctuality. A sign of true stud potential. And you just know a punctual stud like him is *bound* to fall for a desperate psycho like me."

JACK GLANCED AT HIS WATCH and rang the doorbell again. No answer. Should he just walk in? *No.* Any informality on his part was a bad idea after his last encounter with Val. Sure, Valerie was shameless, and he was perverse enough to enjoy that about her.

But it was his own behavior that had him kicking himself now. Talk about overreaction. He felt like an idiot.

When he had first read that damn "funeral" announcement, he'd felt a tickle of nerves down his spine. Then welcome anger and suspicion had kicked in and he'd huffed and fumed down the street to confront the little manipulator.

And that was when he'd blown it. He was worse than Val or even Lillian at her melodramatic best. Well, hell, he'd found the woman lying on the floor with a blood-soaked bullet hole in her dress—when he'd just finished reading a virtual death threat against her. How else could he have reacted? He was a detective and an ex-cop. His first instinct was to protect.

Not that he'd reacted like a cop. He hadn't even checked the "body" for a damn pulse. Nope. Just panicked like some gullible, lovesick fool. And even worse, Val had picked up on it. The last thing he wanted.

Why couldn't he, just once, react to the woman with logic and cool composure? On any given day, Val could make him want to shout, laugh, shake her senseless or drag her off to bed. It was all just too much, too soon, and he didn't want any part of it. Hell, he knew better than to trust strong emotions—others' or his own. They'd twisted his tail before and he had no intention of repeating the experience.

Especially with yet another beautiful woman whose actions sprang from mixed motives. He was too smart for that.

Taking another stab at the doorbell, Jack scowled at his watch, then pounded on the door. If Val had staged this encounter, she was taking too damn many chances in waiting to answer her door. The only reason he'd even come was to prove a point. Val had sicced her aunt on him via the phone and he still stung from the way Lillian had questioned his ethics the other day. *Val*, in need of anyone's protection? Ha! Still, he wanted points for showing up when any fool could see—

The door swung open.

"Don't say it." Val challenged him with a look.

Jack blinked. "Hello?"

"Okay, you can say *that*." She grinned impishly.

"Took you long enough to answer." A thought suddenly occurred to him and he leaned on the doorbell again. No sound. "Well, that explains it."

"The doorbell's not working?" Val frowned. "Something else I need to fix. I'll have to put a sign out until then."

"There's a thought. So what wasn't I supposed to say?" He stepped past her into the foyer.

"That psycho Valerie's using another ploy to get you into her mercenary, not to mention *lascivious*, clutches." Val waggled her eyebrows. "I'm not. Lillian was supposed to squeeze you for recommendations only and thus spare you my scheming ways."

"So she schemed instead?"

"To ask you over here? Of course." Val motioned him into her office. "I think she can't help sticking her nose in other people's business, though, so try to go easy on her." Val spoke the last in a raised voice, obviously intending to be overheard.

Looking up from her magazine, Lillian slipped her glasses off and tucked them in her hair. "Jack. Welcome. Thank you for coming so quickly. And, yes, I'm the little schemer who wouldn't let Val hide her embarrassed self when she had nothing to be embarrassed about. We really do need your advice. Val wants to update the security system around here, and we thought you'd know a lot more about that kind of thing than we do."

Jack glanced from one to the other, not completely convinced, then shrugged philosophically. "Security's a good idea, regardless of your circumstances. If this system's as old as the one in my office building when I took it over, then I'm sure it does need updating."

Val gave him a rueful look just as the phone rang. "It's probably older. Just let me get the phone quick and then I'll show you around."

While Val dealt with what sounded like a vendor, he glanced discreetly at her desk. A phone book lay open, with an entry for an insurance agent circled. When Val hung up the phone, he glanced up. "Ready?" he asked.

"Let's go."

"Just don't forget to call insurance about that claim."

Val glanced back at her aunt's reminder. "Right, thanks. I'll call this afternoon." Lillian went back to her reading.

Together, Jack and Val toured the downstairs and basement, checking all doors and windows. Then they headed outside for a look at the gate and a review of her usual security procedures.

Once they'd viewed everything to Jack's satisfaction, Val led him back to her office. "So what do you think?"

"I think you need to update the place yesterday."

"That bad, huh?" Val grimaced.

"Worse."

She nodded. "Okay. Recommendations? Referrals?"

He gestured with a shoulder. "I and another guy could handle all of it for you if you want. You'd only pay cost."

"Really?" Val brightened. A neighbor—which made him utterly accountable—and at cost! Her mercenary little heart just went pitty-pat at the thought. A little additional pitty or pat might be attributed to the inner vision of Jack hard at manual labor. Talk about a coup. "Jack, that would be wonderful. I didn't even know you did this stuff."

"I don't, but he does. I've been known to assist from

time to time, though." He cleared his throat. "It wouldn't hurt if you passed the word around about my friend, though. He's good, but he's new to the business."

She studied him with interest. "Another ex-cop?"

"Retired cop, actually. My dad."

She smiled a little. "Really. So your dad's retired. And you recently quit the police force yourself. Any connection?"

"No." His frown discouraged further questions.

"I'm just curious."

"So. About the security job. Do we have a deal?"

"Definitely. When can you start? Sometime yesterday, maybe?" She eyed him hopefully.

"Something like that. Let me give my dad a call and see how soon he can fit you in."

"I appreciate it." Not wanting him to get up and leave just yet, she gave him a casually inquiring look. "So. Any other notes show up on your doorstep?"

"*Should* they have?" His voice was all challenge.

"I wouldn't know."

He nodded. Not in agreement, just digesting her response. "Your aunt seemed a little upset about the notes."

"It's just in her nature to see crime and murder in every situation."

"Well, this wasn't exactly a typical situation. I'll give her that much. Not everyone receives notes threatening death."

Val rolled her eyes. "Whatever." Death threats. She just *had* to bring up a sore subject of a tangent. Good move, Val.

"It wouldn't hurt you to take a few precautions with your own safety. Just in case."

"What? Avoid getting a paper cut just in case someone laced those envelopes with poison?"

"How creative of you." Jack spoke without inflection.

"Goes with the territory. But I was joking, you know. They're just notes."

"I suppose. Still, you should pay more attention to locking doors and being aware of your surroundings. It doesn't hurt and these days, you really can't be too careful."

No. Could that be...*concern* she was hearing? In her dreams, maybe. The man was a former cop. Handing out safety tips was second nature to him. Like offering a weird but bleeding stranger a sterile bandage. "I appreciate the concern, Jack, but I already take reasonable precautions. I have no intention of playing terrified little victim for *anybody*—muggers, robbers or note-writing little punks." She smiled sweetly. "Thanks to professional research, I've learned hundreds of ways to kill a person. Knowledge can be so empowering."

He gave her a wry look that was half-serious. "Anyone ever tell you you're scary?"

"Well, there was this one guy who called me a psycho." She shook her head, feigning a woebegone air. "It's tragic, you know. I keep lobbing my poor vulnerable heart at him, but he's just too terrified to date me."

"You got that right."

Val laughed outright. "Oh, Jack. One of these days, I swear you'll be on your knees begging me for that date."

"You may be right, Val, but today's not that day."

"Another day, then?" She folded her hands and rested her chin on them. "Ah, hope at last." She sighed as though yearning. All right, so the yearning was only partly feigned. Infatuation could be so undignified.

"Whatever gets you through, babe."

The office door swung open. "Valerie, I'm really sorry I couldn't—Oh, hello." The stunning brunette smiled at Jack.

He let his gaze slide down the woman's svelte body, then back up again. Scarlet fingernails, pouty lips, sophisticated hair and makeup. Sequins. This woman would wear sequins. He regarded her cautiously.

Valerie sighed. "Simone. I thought you called in sick."

Simone glanced at her boss, her features drooping for a moment. "It's true. I didn't feel well at all earlier." She shifted her gaze back to Jack and her smile grew wide again. "But I might have made the effort if—"

"If you were more dedicated to your *job*?" Valerie spoke sweetly, her eyes flashing with temper.

"I'm dedicated. I just don't work well when I have a headache." Simone continued to study Jack. He felt like a bug pinned to a board for observation and prolonged torture.

"A headache. That's too bad. Ever heard of aspirin?" Valerie spoke crisply. Simone's attention never wavered from Jack. "Obviously not. Simone, I'll need to discuss this with you *after* my meeting." She gave her a pointed stare.

"After your meeting. Certainly, Valerie. I'll be all yours then." Simone's purring tone and the gaze she still leveled at Jack implied she wanted to be all *his*—anytime, anywhere. After a moment, she turned and glided back out of the room, shutting the door behind her.

Jack turned to Valerie. "Your actress?"

"Yes." Her smile was icy. "Although I think she'd much rather be *your* actress."

For the first time since the brunette had entered the room, Jack relaxed enough to smile just a little.

Valerie ignored him.

Still savoring the unexpected power shift, Jack brought the discussion back to business. A quick call to his dad proved he was available as soon as the next day, which pleased Val but left Jack with mixed feelings. His idiot side looked forward to seeing the woman again tomorrow, but his less-idiot side knew prolonged contact with the woman was dangerous to his remaining brain cells. One by one, they self-destructed with every moment he spent around her.

"Well, I guess that'll do it. I'll see you tomorrow, Val."

She stood up. "I couldn't interest you in a strictly business lunch with me today?"

"I already have one of those lined up with a client, but thanks." He followed as Val led him to the door, where he nodded a farewell to Lillian in the foyer and left.

As the door swung shut after him, Val turned back to her aunt. "Security arranged and set for installation tomorrow."

"Fast work." Lillian nodded her approval.

Val smiled a little to herself. "As it happens, Jack and his dad—who also happens to be a former cop but who now runs a security business—will be installing it. At cost."

"Now I'm really impressed." Lillian's smile widened. "So we'll see the delicious detective again tomorrow?"

"Looks like it."

"Good. Don't waste your opportunities, Val. Pounce."

"*Lillian.*" Valerie sent her aunt a half-annoyed, half-entertained look. "It's not pouncing time. The man already thinks I'm half psycho."

"Well, don't wait too long. When's the last time you had a date, anyway? You need some romance in your life." She nodded decisively. "And if not the sexy detective, then I highly recommend you take some other, ill-advised secret lover. It would be so good for you. In fact, I'd recommend taking that studly gardener of yours to bed, except I think he's underage."

Valerie stared. A wild fling with her *teenage landscaper*?

At Val's continued silence, Lillian raised her chin virtuously. "Scoff if you must, but life's too short to forego romantic opportunity. Use it or lose it, darling."

Val shook her head slowly. "And Jack calls *me* scary."

3

"So you're Jack's dad." Valerie smiled flirtatiously at Robert Harrison. While Jack worked on a lock in another room, she would get acquainted with the elder Mr. Harrison and work on solving her own personal mystery.

The man grunted and looked over his shoulder at her. Hazel eyes much like his son's blinked at her then crinkled attractively at the corners. The man smiled. Momentarily surprised out of her fact-finding intentions, Valerie stared. Father and son resembled each other so closely. She just knew that's exactly how Jack would look if he ever relaxed enough to really smile at her.

"I thought we'd already established the family relationship, young lady. If you want to ask questions, just ask 'em. I'll answer if I can."

Valerie blinked to clear her vision, then flashed her most beguiling grin. "All right. Jack tells me you're a retired policeman."

"That's right. I put in my thirty years with the Chicago Police Department, then retired my badge." He turned back to the door and unscrewed the ancient knob.

"That's impressive."

He shrugged. "It's what I did. Now I do this."

"So what brought you to St. Louis?"

"Jack moved here, and with his mom gone, he's my only family. I followed him out here—to his everlasting regret, no doubt." Robert gave her a mischievous look.

She laughed softly. "Well, I think it serves him right."

"How so?"

"Hey, he followed in your footsteps first, didn't he? His choice of career?"

"Oh, sure. He talked about joining the police force from the time he was just a little guy."

"I'm surprised he quit, then."

The humor left his face. "That's something you'll have to take up with him."

She sighed.

He grinned. "Thought it was worth a try, huh?"

With a wry smile of her own, Valerie folded her arms across her chest and leaned against the wall to watch him. "No offense, but your son's a tough guy to figure out."

"And you just love to figure out his kind of mystery." He sent her a shrewd glance before turning back to the door.

She frowned. "Well, yes, but not— I mean, sure, I'm curious, but it's not a malicious kind of curious. If you know what I mean."

He grinned again, not taking his attention from the piece of old metal he was prying loose. "Oh, I know what you mean."

Valerie narrowed her eyes, realizing from his tone that Jack's dad did know exactly what she meant. She hadn't intended to be so obvious about her interest. "So what do you suggest?"

"Give him time. He's real cautious about giving anything away." He set down the screwdriver and faced her squarely. "It's been a while since he focused on his personal life. And I have to say he didn't do such a good job of it the last time. I wouldn't be surprised if he was clumsy and slow about it for a while yet. Be patient with him."

She nodded thoughtfully. *The last time.* Interesting.

"So why don't you take this drill to my son and worm around in his brain instead. He has your answers, not me."

"Oh, you had a few of them." She accepted the tool gingerly, then offered him a wink and a smile. "Thanks."

He just shook his head in a familiar expression of exasperation that made her laugh.

"Whenever you need a break, go find my aunt in the kitchen. She's made cookies and lemonade for you and Jack. A 'humble salute to our local heroes,' I believe she said." Val dropped her voice conspiratorially. "And she almost *never* makes cookies anymore so you don't want to miss this."

"Yes, ma'am. I'll do that. Thanks."

Still smiling, she obediently set off in search of the younger Mr. Harrison. First stop: an attic bedroom, where she'd last seen him working.

"Valerie." Kneeling before a half-open bedroom window, Jack spoke over his shoulder without turning around.

He'd known it was her without even looking. An intriguing detail to file away. She set the drill down next to him. "You wanted me?" The lilt in her voice added mocking weight to the double entendre.

He barely glanced her way as he slid the window shut and picked up the drill.

"Gee, and until a moment ago, I was going to offer to install a new doorbell if you wanted it."

"You were?" The man sounded downright playful. A girl could almost hope.

"Yeah, I *was*." Emphasis on the past tense.

"Then, as appreciative as I'm sure I *would* have been, I'd have to say no, thank you. I special-ordered a new doorbell that came with an intercom system. The deal included installation, but it'll be another week before it comes in." She chuckled evilly. "But you've *got* to hear this bell's chime."

He sat back on his heels. "Yeah?"

"Spoo-ky. Like you're visiting Count Dracula's house. It's great. I can't wait to get it installed. Just think of Halloween night." She laughed, already anticipating. Kids came well out of their way to check out her haunted house on the creepiest night of the year. She considered it her duty not to disappoint them—in tricks or in treats.

He gave her a curious look. "I bet you're the hit of the neighborhood come Halloween."

"I try."

He nodded thoughtfully. "Goes with the ghosts."

"No surprise there." She frowned at a nagging thought. "A lot of things do these days."

"Huh?"

"Go with the ghosts. Or at least the klepto bride ghost."

"Translation?"

She sighed. "I have a sapphire necklace I can't find. It was my mother's and now it's missing."

"And this is connected to your ghosts." Jack looked skeptical.

"Ah, the cynical detective is back. Yes, it has to do with our ghosts. One of them likes to steal blue things. Or, rather, borrow them."

"Really. So tell me about these ghosts. What all have they *borrowed* so far?"

"Only the bride borrows things. You know—'something

old, something new, something borrowed, something *blue*'? Legend has it that the woman died while still in pursuit of blue. On her wedding day. Isn't that wild?"

"Wild, all right. So now you have a sapphire necklace missing?"

"Well, yeah. I wouldn't really worry about it except lately our bride hasn't been giving stuff back. She usually only takes one thing at a time, and nothing goes missing until I've located whatever she took last. But so far I'm still missing a dandy little blue fountain pen, a blue glass mug and now the sapphire necklace." She frowned, then shrugged. "It's probably someplace I just haven't looked yet. She puts things back in the oddest places sometimes."

Jack set the drill down and stood up. "Just how valuable is this necklace?"

"I'm not sure, really. It's not blatantly luxe, but it could probably go for a decent price at auction. Monetarily, it's no big deal. It's insured. I just like the piece, and it was my mother's so there's sentimental value attached to it. She wore it in her first and only film."

"Her *film*?"

"My mom was an actress."

"Really." He sounded mildly intrigued. "How about that? And she wore that necklace in a movie." His eyebrows lowered. "In that case, maybe the necklace is worth more than you know."

"Always the detective." She smiled, dismissing his concern. "So how are the locks coming along?"

He glanced behind him at the window and then at the door, both sporting shiny new pieces of sturdy metal. "Fine. Dad and I should be done and out of your hair in three hours, tops."

She fluttered her lashes. "Don't rush off on my account."

He just shook his head, eyes gleaming with reluctant humor.

But he was true to his word. Less than three hours later, she was walking him to the door, contemplating the best way to ask the man out—again—when the front door opened before she could touch it.

Valerie looked up in surprise. "William. Are you finished already? That's great."

William, a truly buff young man of about seventeen or so, smiled, but it disappeared when his gaze slipped past her to include Jack. Jack studied the teenager with quiet intensity, but didn't smile and didn't comment.

Taking the clipboard from William, she signed it, then dug through her pocket for an appropriate tip. "The yard and gardens look beautiful. Thanks for all your hard work." He blushed as usual, she noted in amusement. "I don't know what we'd do without you."

"No problem, Ms. Longstreet." He shot an oddly triumphant look over her shoulder at Jack. "I'll see you Tuesday, then."

"Perfect." She waved briefly, then turned back to Jack. He towered closer than she'd thought and unexpectedly slapped a hand against the door, closing it after William.

"Jack?" Steadying herself with both hands against a hard chest, she looked up with a frown to encounter narrowed eyes and a clenched jaw. He was mad at her again. She sighed. "What now?"

"You can't be that naive, Valerie. William the *landscaper*? Isn't he a little young?" Jack smiled, his lips tight and anything but amused.

Baffled, Valerie glanced over her shoulder, mentally recalling the young man to memory, then returned her attention to Jack. "I think he's in his late teens. That's old enough to be responsible. He's polite and very good at what he does."

Jack lowered his voice to a bad-tempered growl. "How good?"

Taken aback, she studied his face for a moment. The conclusion she drew both amused and annoyed her; it appeared the good detective needed another lesson in false leads. She peered up at him through lowered lashes. "Oh, he's exceptional. William's a detail man, and you know how women appreciate that. Customer satisfaction means just *everything* to him."

"Really." Jack moved closer, his bulk crowding her.

"Oh, yes." She held her ground and felt incredibly feline. "He loves the heat, he's very strong and he can keep at it for hours and hours. Ah, the stamina of youth."

Jack's lips twitched.

She smiled, slow and wide and taunting.

"Oh, but you are a witch, Valerie Longstreet."

"So I've been told. What a shame, huh?"

He sighed, draping his arms loosely around her neck. "You know how to push my buttons, that's for sure." His arms felt good. Just that little bit of voluntary contact from a man who normally avoided anything of the sort around her.

"It's hard not to when you shove them in my face like that." Sliding her palms higher, Val brushed a fingertip inside his open collar and tipped her head back to meet his eyes. "So you think I like to take young lovers, do you?"

His arms tightened as he scowled down at her. "I'm sure he'd be more than happy if you did."

"Are you serious?" Valerie was incredulous. "He's a kid, Jack. Get real."

He held her gaze. "He's a teenager with hormones raging like no woman can possibly understand. Nothing's hornier than a seventeen-year-old looking at a sexy woman in a short skirt."

"Short skirt? This is perfectly reason—" His lips captured hers, muffling her words and chasing them deliriously from memory.

Lord, but the man could kiss. She groaned wholeheartedly approval and he slowed to savor. Firm lips plucked at hers, lingering and sliding. Unabashedly hungry. She sighed, her breath mingling with his as she sank all of her senses into the experience. Lovely.

He leaned into her, pressing her against the oak door, her breasts crushed against his chest. Feeling drunk on sensation, she tipped her head back against the polished wood. He nipped at her lower lip before sliding his mouth to her chin and then down to her long, exposed throat. Lightly, so lightly, he raked her skin with his teeth, the sandy texture of his jaw buzzing along her nerve endings.

She shivered. He exhaled roughly.

Who knew? Tall, sexy and reserved was absolute dynamite under the pleated khakis and conservative shirt. The man would be a powerhouse in bed. It was enough to make a woman feel weak. Even inadequate. How long had it been since she last—

"Jack." She gasped, skin tingling riotously from a tiny bite low on her neck. Knees weakening, she slid lower against the door.

But he lifted her to her toes and slid his lips along the delicate ridge of collarbone, gliding over the fluttery pulse just above it. She felt his mouth curve as he gave a little hum of satisfaction before he continued farther down, exploring soft skin along the edge of her scoop-neck sweater.

"You're killing me."

"Shh." He sounded almost angry, his breath heating the tops of her breasts and riding the cleft between them. Ducking, he buried his face in her cleavage. His movements sensuous, he rubbed his cheeks and jaw between the swells of her breasts, inhaling her scent. His utter abandon tugged at her heart. So unexpected. She burrowed her fingers into the silky hair at his nape, while he kissed—

The *click-click* of high heels interrupted, and Jack raised his head just as Simone stepped into the hallway. She halted at the sight of them.

And, oh, what an incriminating sight it was, Valerie thought ruefully. She cleared her throat. "Did you need something, Simone?"

The actress raised a carefully groomed eyebrow. "Not as much as you do. Dare I suggest you get a room?"

A little surprised at the venom behind the woman's words, Valerie stared back at her. "I wouldn't recommend it."

"You're the boss." Simone flashed a knowing smile, paused, then sauntered down the hall away from them.

Jack inhaled deeply and released it almost gingerly. "Wow."

Valerie looked at him and laughed, dazzled anew by the hot memory of his kisses. "You're not kidding. Who knew?" Good grief, she was still trembling and felt as though she could burst into flames or song at any moment.

"I suspected." His gaze dropped to her mouth and he traced a finger over her lip. "I've wanted you since I first laid eyes on you."

"You hide it well." She stared up into his eyes.

"God knows I tried." He dropped his hand back to her shoulder, sliding it beneath her hair as he met her gaze. He looked troubled, even angry. Certainly brooding. "It's not working, though. I can't stop thinking about you."

She moved closer. "I want to see you. Tonight. Take me to dinner or a movie. Anything."

"I shouldn't. This is such a bad idea. You and me, getting involved?" He shook his head, staring at her mouth again. "It could get so damn messy."

She smiled and tilted her chin higher. "I don't know about messy. But it does sound pretty good right now."

"Yeah. Damn good." He closed his eyes on a grimace. "What the hell. I'll take you out."

Laughter bubbled up, but she bit it back. "How *romantic*. Why, I feel all weak and fluttery inside."

His mouth curved at the corners, a flash of the reticent Jack who had intrigued her these past weeks. "I'll pick you up at seven."

She lowered her lashes and smiled up at him. "It's a date."

He gave her a short, hard kiss, then stepped back. "Lock up behind me."

She nodded, watching him leave. Once the door closed behind him, she dropped the sultry pose and sagged against the wall. "Wow. Damn. *Really* wow." She blinked. "Now what?"

She glanced around, only to realize she was half swooning against the front door, for all the world to witness. *Classy image, Val.* Carefully, she picked her way back to her office and closed the door behind her.

Once there, she tried to repair her appearance. The goose bumps and melting feeling kept coming and going as she relived the past several minutes. *Jack*. This was more than she'd expected. And obviously, more of a problem for him than she'd guessed it would be. But they had a date tonight.

Then she flashed to a memory of Simone interrupting them, her dark eyes expressing a distinctly womanly fury. *Dare I suggest you get a room?* Valerie groaned and left to find Simone.

She found the actress in her usual pose: relaxing on the patio with a manicure set, a mirror and a dog-eared stack of fashion magazines on the table in front of her. A slave to fashion, Simone was constantly snipping at dainty bits of hair or redoing her nails to fit the latest styles. She was actually quite skilled at it.

For now, those skillfully fussing hands were still. A script for the next whodunit had been tossed carelessly on the ground, and Simone had tipped that gorgeous head back to absorb the slanted autumn sunshine. Valerie paused in front of her, a shadow blocking the sun, and Simone's eyes fluttered open.

"Let's talk." Valerie turned and strode back into the building. After a moment, she heard the scrape of a chair and then the unhurried click of heels following in her wake.

Valerie closed her office door behind Simone and gestured to the couch. Then she leaned against her desk and folded her arms. "So let's have it."

Simone shrugged delicately and crossed her legs. "Let's have what? An apology? All right. I'm sorry I interrupted you and the good detective getting it on in the foyer."

Valerie smiled coolly. "I accept your apology. Now tell me why you keep looking at me like you want to tear my hair out."

The woman's smile slipped and her hands tightened into fists. "So maybe I wanted him, too. You just got to him before I could."

Valerie frowned. "That's all? This is really about Jack?"

"It's enough, don't you think? You were poaching."

Valerie studied the woman. Poaching? Really? Maybe if she just waited for the punch line... But, no. Simone seemed honestly lost in her simmering melodrama of lust and betrayal. Valerie inhaled and tried for patience. "Look. I'm sorry you had to witness what you did. And I'm sorry if you're disappointed that there's something personal developing between Jack and me. But you just met the man. Frankly, it doesn't look to me like you have any claim on him."

Simone glared. She radiated emotion. Presence. Abandoning the position of Strong and Righteous, Simone now gave a beautiful rendering of Angry and Mortally Wounded. "I wanted him and you knew it. I've been watching him for a while now, waiting for the right moment to approach him. But you had to keep throwing yourself at him. You stole him from me."

With an effort, Valerie kept her mouth closed, tried to construct some semblance of a rational argument. So she was going to use reason? To combat *unreasonable?*

Gee, as if *that* didn't have failure written all over it. Actors and their temperamental flights of fancy. What could you do? Still, was some loose connection to reality too much to expect? She groaned inwardly, knowing she had no choice but to give doomed reason a try.

"Okay, Simone, if you were already attracted to Jack, I guess I can understand why you might be upset right now. But what about Jack? Did he ever return your feelings? He's always given me the impression that he was unattached. Fair game, so to speak." Valerie blinked, absolutely refusing to believe she'd just said that. Poaching...fair game. Talk about belabored metaphors.

But, really, she thought on sudden—perhaps desperate—inspiration. This whole scene just smacked of overacting. Could it be part of some elaborate hoax? That was possible, she supposed. Her employees were a fun-loving group, fully capable of setting the boss up for a good punch line. Why, just last week, Mandy, Lillian, the guys and even her new chef had—

Valerie sighed. Still there was no denying that she'd never considered Simone and herself as being on joking terms.

And Simone did *not* look entertained right now. "I let him know how I felt. Or I would have, but I was waiting for my cue. I wasn't going to jump him in the foyer." Simone eyed her boss contemptuously. *Like you did*, she might as well have said.

Nope, Simone was not joking. And insubordination was rearing its nasty head. Valerie really hated playing the heavy, but Simone was crossing some big, ugly lines, and things were deteriorating rapidly.

She smiled coolly at Simone. "I guess I lack your subtlety. But that's beside the point now. Has it occurred to you lately that I am still your boss and as such, I'm deserving of some respect, or at least a little diplomacy, whatever you might think of me? You don't have to agree with everything I say or do, but a little common courtesy—"

Simone's temper flared. "So I quit." She launched off the couch and stormed out of the office. The door rebounded against the wall behind her.

"Over a man you considered *prey*?" Her words echoing

in the empty room, Valerie stared after Simone, feeling deflated and more than a little confused.

YEP, NO DOUBT ABOUT IT. He was a self-destructive idiot, Jack decided. Not only had he agreed to go out with one hell of a dangerous woman—a man only had so many disposable brain cells, when all was said and done—but he also couldn't concentrate on work. All he could think about was Val.

How had he gotten so caught up in her so quickly? The woman was a complete flake. The vampy mannerisms she used—and he was all but certain now that she only pulled them out for play and pretend, like a playful imp assuming the vampy Miss Scarlet role in that whodunit board game. Movie. Whatever. It was all games, anyway. And then there was the teasing and talk of ghosts—

Ghosts. Yeah, that was a shocker. Val was so down-to-earth when it came to business, but she really seemed to believe in those ghosts of hers. Kleptomaniac ghosts, no less.

He frowned. The klepto part really nagged at him, too. A mug, a pen, no problem. Anyone could shrug off something cheap like that as easily misplaced and replaced. The necklace, though, was interesting. Good thing it was insured. In his experience, when valuable things went missing, there was usually someone who profited from the loss. One way or another.

Jack frowned. Then he remembered yesterday's encounter in Val's office, glancing at her phone book while she took a call. She had circled a listing for an insurance company.

Profit…one way or another.

Was she filing a claim against the necklace? If so, what would she tell the insurance company? That a *ghost* took it?

No insurance company would buy such a hokey explanation.

He closed his eyes, seeking objectivity. Take a necklace. Take a smart woman with a struggling new business blaming the necklace's disappearance on a ghost, and then filing an insurance claim. Setting up a pattern of things "stolen." Logically speaking, something else could be stolen later? *And subsequently reported to the insurance company.*

But why would a smart woman blame a missing necklace on a ghost? Maybe when it disappeared she couldn't bring herself to blame a real person? Because she knew no one had really taken it? *Because it never went missing in the first place?*

Insurance fraud?

Jack opened his eyes. No. He was reaching now. That was a big old leap to take, from missing necklace to ghost to insurance fraud.

Still, the gap between missing gems and insurance fraud wasn't so great. The unlikely addition of a ghost, however... Actually, it was *so* unlikely, that someone like Val, with her beauty and eloquence, could make a believable case for truth being stranger than fiction. That would be almost ingenious.

And, if the stranger-than-fiction explanation didn't work, she could just fake surprised dismay as she "confronted" the inevitable possibility that she might have been robbed by a living, breathing person. "Why it had *never* occurred to her and..." Yeah, that was the mark of Valerie. Ingenious and disingenuous. Slick combination.

Jack groaned. And he had a date with her tonight.

Bad plan. No matter how he looked at it—whether the woman was innocent or guilty—dating Val was a bad, bad idea.

FORCING HERSELF to set aside thoughts of Simone, Val concentrated on more important matters. Like who could take on Simone's role in upcoming mystery productions. And what the hell Val would wear on her date with Jack tonight. She didn't know where they were going or what they were doing.

But knowing Jack... Val smiled. The guy liked his khakis, his polos, his reserve and his tradition. Dinner and a movie, she'd bet. She wondered if she could talk him into a little tongue tango in the darkened theater. Wow, but the man could kiss.

Smiling at a not-too-distant memory of those kisses, she touched a hand to her bare collarbone. The lucky sapphires. She really wanted to wear those sapphires tonight. Damn.

"Val, darling." Lillian poked her head in the door and Val opened her eyes.

"Mmm?"

Lillian looked a little hesitant, glanced behind her, then walked in. "I just got off the phone, dear. I tried to stall him and get him to talk to you, but—"

Val groaned. "Jack. He's backing out on me."

"I'm afraid so, darling. He said something came up at the last minute."

"Is that so." Val narrowed her eyes.

Lillian gave her a sympathetic smile. "Well...there's always the gardener?"

"Hello? He's a *minor*."

"Beggars can't be choosers," Lillian responded in singsong.

Val scowled at her aunt, who just regarded her with a calm smile. "Well, I'm not a beggar yet." Val turned back to her desk, thoughtful, then thumbed through the phone book until she found what she was looking for.

Harrison Security Systems.

Smiling, she picked up the phone and dialed. "Mr. Harrison, how are you?"

A man chuckled. "Please. Call me Robert. I've seen your locks. We're as good as friends now."

Val laughed. "I knew I liked you. So, Robert, about that mysterious son of yours…"

"JACK HARRISON. As I live and breathe."

Startled, Jack straightened on his bar stool and glanced over his shoulder. Valerie. Of course. "Hi, Val."

She smiled and strode across the bar to his side. "Scaredy-cat. It was just a *date*. I don't even *like* orange blossoms."

"Like I told Lillian—"

"I heard." She waved it off and slid onto the stool next to him. Her silky gold blouse clung, smoothed and slid over high breasts and a tiny waist as she set a handbag on the bar and crossed one smooth leg over the other. "You canceled our date tonight because 'something came up.' So, the bar stool came up and hit you in the butt, did it?" Her lashes swept low as she glanced at said butt, before meeting his gaze again.

Jack couldn't suppress a half laugh in surprise.

She nodded, suspicions obviously confirmed. But she wasn't angry? "I'm not surprised. Your dad warned me you were a relationship weenie."

"He said what?"

"But don't make a habit of lying to me to cancel dates." She raised her eyebrows. "If you want to cancel a date because you're a weenie, at least have the courage to say so."

"Val—"

"Unless it wasn't cold feet that had you canceling our date?"

He studied her a moment. "We don't know each other very well."

"Not for lack of trying—at least on *my* part."

He gave her a speculative look. "I'm not so sure about that." *The vampy stuff. The necklace. The insurance claim? Fraud?* "Ever find your necklace?"

She paused at the change of subject. "No, actually." Then frowned. "I really wanted to wear it tonight, too." She glanced at him, a small smile tugging at her lips.

He nodded, still studying her.

"Care to buy a girl a drink?"

He eyed her with reluctant amusement. "Is this a date?"

"Of course not. This is just a sleazy pickup." She gave him a laughing look.

That startled him a little. "Really?"

Now she did laugh. "No. I just wanted to see if I could put that look on your face. It worked." She opened her purse. "And I can buy my own drink. Honestly, I was just teasing."

Feeling both rude and asinine about his own behavior, he beckoned to the bartender. "My treat. What can I get you?"

"Just a cola, please. Thanks."

He nodded and ordered for her. He wasn't sure what he'd expected her to order, but the nonalcoholic beverage was a bit of a surprise. Maybe a fancy flavored martini? Or something like a screwdriver? Hip city chick or old-fashioned vamp, he would have thought. Not teetotaler.

But by now he also knew there was more to the woman than met the eye. He supposed a fair man wouldn't have jumped to conclusions about insurance fraud, either.

Maybe. Very likely, one of her guests had just lifted the necklace from her.

And Jack had to admit that, as Val had said, he probably had the worst cold feet of any man. *Relationship weenie.* Ah, yes. He felt like such a man right now.

Lips twisting in self-mockery and minor guilt—sure, he'd jumped to conclusions, but, hey, it was part of his job to be suspicious and cynical—he turned to his "date." "Hungry?"

"Nope. When my date canceled—" she grinned at him "—I grabbed something at the restaurant." She gave him a rueful look. "Seriously, though, I wasn't trying to ambush you."

"Oh, you weren't, huh?"

"Well, okay, I was. But I wanted to talk to you, not force you to date me when you obviously didn't want to."

"I didn't say I didn't want to." He offered the truth reluctantly.

"You didn't?" She studied him a moment before narrowing her eyes shrewdly. "And I'll bet that was exactly the problem. You didn't *want* to want to go out with me."

Bull's-eye. Although a more accurate statement would be that he wanted to date her too much. Mild attraction he could deal with. Brainless fascination was too much to handle.

They drank in silence for a few moments. Val eyed him, still trying to decide what her reaction ought to be. She didn't like being stood up. But she liked Jack.

"So." He cleared his throat. "How's the food here, anyway?"

"I've heard it's wonderful." She leaned toward him conspiratorially. "Just don't tell my chef. I'd hate to lose her to a jealous hissy fit, after just firing my other chef. God knows I don't want to go through that again. A chefless restaurant is a nightmare, let me tell you."

Jack's lips twitched and he frowned, as though recalling a vague memory. "Your *other* chef. Yeah, I heard about that. Not exactly the poster child for kitchen hygiene, huh?"

She closed her eyes. "It wasn't pretty. I was just trying to give the man the privacy he said was necessary for his creativity. So I stayed out of his kitchen as much as possible. He was good. A very creative cook. He just...well, the roast duck..." She shrugged helplessly.

"Ah. The duck. You know, poultry will get you every time." He shook his head in feigned regret.

"You're impossible."

"If I am, it only serves you right." He gave her a wry look.

"Me? Why?"

"Yes, you. For weeks now, you've flirted ruthlessly with me. As hard as I tried to resist, you just kept at it. Taunting and teasing until I thought I'd internally combust."

She winced.

He frowned. "What? What did I say?"

She forced a smile. "Not you. Am I really a tease?"

"Of course you're a tease." He looked baffled. "An excellent one. Hell, it's part of your charm."

She groaned. "Charming, all right."

"Why? What's wrong?"

"Let's just say I'm a little unsettled by something that happened earlier today. Another ex-employee. And the *ex* part is only a few hours old."

"Who?"

"Simone. I had a disturbing conversation with her. Right after she busted us."

"Really."

She nodded thoughtfully. "Simone says I was poaching."

Jack stared, wide-eyed. "Poaching? Who? Because of *me*? But I don't— Hell, you couldn't possibly mean—"

Oddly enough, Jack's complete bafflement served to restore her balance and sense of humor. "Oh, but I do, Jack. And, frankly, I'm surprised at you. I had no idea you and Simone had grown so close in so short a time. I don't like to share."

Jack stared at her. "But I just met her a day ago. Maybe two days? Hell, I've never even spoken to the woman."

Valerie choked on her laughter. Jack was almost sweating with discomfort. Poor man. Beset with predatory women. "I don't know, Jack. She seemed pretty convinced. Maybe it was one of those mysterious subliminal things."

He stared at her, wide eyes finally narrowing as he obviously realized Val was entertaining herself at his expense. "Right. *Subliminal*."

She laughed, then shook her head. "I swear, it was the weirdest thing, though. I honestly think she was just practicing her acting talents on me today."

"Why would she do that? She just lost a decent job because of it."

"I've suspected all along that she didn't really want to be working at the inn. You know, the artist's struggle between the need for a steady income and a desire to pursue the craft unconditionally."

Jack still looked confused.

Val clarified. "She wanted to perform on Broadway or be a hotdog movie star. Not play murderers and victims in my little theater. I would bet she jumped at the excuse to leave this job, and pulled a weird temperamental artist on me to get me to fire her."

"Is that a technical term?"

She shrugged. "Just one I invented to suit my own purposes. It works well in the odd situation."

"Whatever gets you through."

She grinned and stood up. "Well, thanks for the drink. And for humoring my ambush. I should get going now."

He rose to his feet. "You walked, didn't you?" She walked everywhere. "Let me give you a ride home. It's dark."

She paused, then nodded. "All right. Thanks."

He followed her out the door. "So how did you find me, anyway?"

She gave him a mysterious look. "A little detective work."

"Really." He drew the word out as though mildly impressed.

"Yep. I called your daddy." Mystery faded to cheesy grin.

He shook his head as he unlocked her car door, obviously entertained again. She was getting good at this. "Rank amateur."

"Sure, but it worked, didn't it?" She met his eyes with a smug little smile, then slid into the seat, waiting while he slammed the door shut.

As Valerie fastened her seat belt, still chuckling a little to herself, she glanced to her left and stilled. A familiar, parchment-colored envelope lay on the driver's seat. She plucked it up as Jack slid behind the wheel.

"Why, Jack, darling, you are a popular man. Me, Simone. And now you've stolen the heart of my own personal 'stalker'?" She held the envelope out to him. "This is addressed to *you*."

4

A SMART DETECTIVE would keep his distance from Valerie Longstreet.

Just like the previous notes—except for the funeral invitation—this message was constructed from cut out scraps of magazines carefully glued into place. Jack stared at the note, frowning. "Looks like somebody doesn't want us together."

"Gee, I needed a private eye to figure that out for me." She raised her chin. "Are you sure it wasn't *your* wussy cold feet, tripping all over themselves to plant this in your car?"

"What?"

"Well, it sure beats 'something came up.'" Mortified and trying to hide it, she spoke the last in a mockingly low timbre. "If you don't want to date me, just say so and *mean* it. I thought we were playing at all this."

She moved to get out of his car, but he grabbed her shoulder and turned her around. "You think *I* set this up? That *I* wrote this note and dropped it onto my own car seat?"

She shrugged carelessly and avoided his gaze. "The door *was* locked. Besides, wouldn't it be great payback for what you think *I* did? Even though I did *not* send you that damn funeral notice? And, even better! You could get me out of your hair, once and for all, without playing the bad guy. A bloodless brush-off."

"Oh, come on, Val. That's ridiculous. I didn't plant this note. I had no idea you were going to be at the bar tonight."

"Who says I was intended to find this thing now? Maybe you were going to drop by the inn later tonight or tomorrow and show it to me then so I'd leave you alone. For your own *safety*, of course. God, that's bad. Just how desperate do you think I am?"

Still grasping her upper arm, Jack leaned his head back and pounded it repeatedly against the headrest. Then, obviously forcing himself to calm, he turned back to her. "For one last time, I did not write this. I did not plant this here."

"So how did it get here?"

He knocked on his window. "I left the window open a crack."

"A former *cop* left his window open. How believable."

Jack groaned feelingly. "I did not *purposely* leave the window open. The damn thing's crooked. I need to get it fixed."

Still suspicious, she leaned across his seat and tried rolling up the window, then rolling it down, and rolling it up again. Sure enough, an oblong triangle of space remained at the top of his window. "All right. I can see that." She sat back. Gave him a suspicious look. "So you didn't write the note? Didn't put it in your seat?"

"I swear."

She plopped back with a huff and stared out the windshield. "Yeah, well, it *would* be an easy way to ditch me. If that's what you wanted. And you sure as hell wanted to ditch me earlier."

"I apologized for that."

"Uh-huh. I still think you have confrontation issues."

He gave her a half-crazed look. "Now, what?"

"Confrontation issues. You'd be surprised how many guys have a hard time confronting women when it comes to romantic issues. Or lack of them."

"I don't have confrontation issues."

"Sure you don't. Oh, wait a minute. That's right. You did confront my aunt and asked *her* to tell *me* that 'something came up.'" Her voice dripping with sarcasm, she gave him a wide-eyed stare intended to provoke.

It worked.

As she turned away, he grabbed her shoulder and tugged her close for a fast, hard kiss. When he pulled back, she gave him a dazed look before her lips parted and curved. *"Jaaaack."*

"Is that confrontational enough for you?"

"I'll say."

"Good." He almost missed the tremble of her chin, her sophisticated cool was that damn good. He wondered what thoughts were flying around inside that brain of hers.

"Like to keep a girl on her toes, do you?"

He forced a frown. "And you enjoy playing with my head way too damn much."

"Me? What about you? Running hot and cold, making and canceling dates, then kissing me senseless. You act like a nervous little virgin."

"Yeah, well, nervous virgin or not—" He groaned. "I take that back. *Not* a nervous little virgin."

She laughed.

"But I'll admit to having mixed feelings about us dating. Until I get them straightened out in my own head, it might be a good idea for us to cool it."

"Fine. Take me home." She gave him an exasperated look. "God knows how you managed to escape nervous little virginity at this rate of romantic progress."

He bit back a chuckle.

"You know, for such a big, strong guy you've got the worst cold feet I've ever encountered." She faced forward in her seat and recrossed her legs. "It's enough to give any girl a complex."

Jack couldn't help smiling a little at the picture she presented—an appealing hybrid of pouting child and annoyed seductress—but he schooled his features before she saw his amusement and killed him for it. A guy could only take so many chances. "Skip the complex, Val. You don't need it."

"I think I will." She raised her nose in the air. "Home, James."

Shaking his head, he pulled out into traffic and traveled the short distance to Longstreet Inn. He made to put the car in Park, but she stopped him. "I can see myself in. Thanks for the drink and the ride." She raised an eyebrow. "It's been interesting."

As she exited the car, he had half an urge—more than half—to call her back, but he stopped himself. Just watched while she disengaged the alarm, waved him goodbye and closed the door.

Jack sighed. She was right about those cold feet. And he was an idiot.

But, damn it, just this afternoon he'd half suspected her of insurance fraud. It would be wrong to get involved with her. Cruel. Duplicitous. Dishonorable, even. He'd been absolutely right to cancel their date. A man had to maintain *some* standards. Even if his libido rejected every last one of them.

Still justifying his logic and actions, he started driving to his own place, but he was too damn restless to go inside just yet. On impulse, he turned his car toward the riverfront with the intent of clearing his head. Maybe walking a little.

After half an hour's worth of driving slowly along the bumpy, cobblestoned streets of Laclede's Landing, watching couples stroll and hop from bar to bar, he still didn't have any answers. Other than time. Once he and Val got to know each other better, he'd know for sure if he could trust her. That much settled in his mind, he finally headed home. It was just coincidence—of course it was—that the route he chose led him right past Longstreet Inn.

As he rounded the corner and headed past her building, he slowed, eyeing the various windows and noting which ones were still lit up. He understood she kept one of the attic rooms as her personal space, but wasn't sure which one. He bet those attic rooms were pretty damn interesting, too. Might even have a secret passageway or two—who knew. These were old buildings and some of them did.

He skimmed his gaze down the building to study the ground-floor windows. All were darkened, but for the entryway. The dim glow of a lamp shone through the door's stained-glass window. As he stared a moment, his car little more than crawling, Jack saw a dark-clad figure crouched low and disappearing around the corner of the building.

Mindful of the missing necklace, Jack slammed the car into Park, shut it off and took off after the shadowy figure.

LONG AFTER SHE'D LOCKED UP for the night, Val wrestled thoughts about Jack and his attitude toward dating her.

Was she that high a risk for a date candidate? Apparently. *Jack* certainly thought so.

As did the note-writing idiot, obviously. First there were vague threats sent to her. Then the funeral notice—amounting to a death threat against her—sent to Jack. Val snorted. *Right. Death threat. I'm sooo scared. Bring it on, buddy.*

Except now the guy was really getting in her way. Warning Jack to stay away from her. As if she needed yet another obstacle between her and getting hot and heavy with the detective.

Just who did this guy think he was kidding with all these melodramatic little messages? Was she supposed to take him *seriously?* Please. Sure, she had an active imagination—it went with the territory—but she liked to think it was grounded in common sense and above-idiot-level intelligence.

Who would really want to hurt her, after all? And why? She didn't have money or power or even a decent sex life to covet. Just dreams. An inn that was heavily in debt. Friends.

So that left her with the adolescent prankster theory. Still, she had to admit that this persistence seemed above and beyond what she would have expected of an adolescent. Unless today's teenagers were blessed with a lot more patience than she'd had as a kid.

Had she unknowingly hurt someone? Offended someone? She'd like to think not, but she was human, after all. Not everyone understood her twisted sense of humor—

"Oh, quit, already." She plopped down into a chair in disgust. Even if she'd offended someone, no faux pas of hers would be bad enough to merit death threats, for Pete's sake. At least, not serious ones. No, it had to be a prank and she was wasting her time trying to look deeper than that.

On that thought, she flipped on the tube. A reality show. She snorted. "What fool would eat slugs for less than a cool million bucks?" She flipped past it to a sitcom repeat, a home-decorating network, a lame movie she'd already seen. Then she settled on a newsy learning channel. "Nothing else on." She tossed the remote onto the bed and settled back to watch.

"...It was a heinous, truly brutal crime that remains unsolved. A death that shocked everyone. The victim was well liked, a good citizen and friend. Who would want to kill her, and in such a gruesome manner? To this day—twenty years later—the victim's neighbors are still finding scraps of clothing, even fragments of bone. And yet the police—"

Click. Eyes wide, Val stood in front of the now-blank television screen, her finger hovering over the Power button. But the images remained fresh in her mind. Bits of clothing. Bone fragments. *Death.* The words echoed in the silent room.

She wished she had a full inn tonight, with voices and people and scattered energy stirring up the old building. As it was, she was alone except for, possibly, Lillian sleeping in her bedroom downstairs. Her aunt always went to bed early, preferring the early-morning hours for writing.

Lillian also believed the inn's ghosts were most active during the wee hours, and she loved the "vibes" she swore they gave off. The writer in her found them inspiring.

Ghosts. More death. Val had heard the stories. A suicide in one of the rooms on the second floor. A healthy man dead of a supposed heart attack in the library. A bride who'd fallen to her death in the basement. Former owners and tenants of the inn had sworn to hearing voices and experiencing strange happenings over the years. All due to ghostly hauntings incited by violent deaths. Would Valerie be next?

"Oh, get a grip." She swung around, nearly slamming her shin into a nightstand, when she heard a scraping noise. Downstairs? Maybe Lillian was just getting home now. But her aunt had never mentioned going out tonight.

What if it was a burglar? Should Val be a responsible little innkeeper and investigate?

"Oh, sure. And this would be the part of the movie where the witless damsel wanders around in the dark, calling out 'Who's there?' then shrieks like an even bigger doofus *just* before she's gutted and dismembered by a psycho with a chain saw. *Ha.* Not *this* female."

Narrowing her eyes and keeping an ear out for further noises, she reached into her nightstand for a flashlight then dug the cell phone out of her purse. "Nope. *This* girl's staying right here. Why look for trouble when you know damn well it's set on finding *you*?" She glanced nervously into every dark corner as she retrieved the baseball bat she kept under her bed.

"Yep. This would be *my* security system." She hefted the bat, seeking some courage in the feel of it, wickedly solid in her hands. "Never, *ever* underestimate the effectiveness of blunt force," she murmured ghoulishly, her nerves taut and her heart hammering as the shuffling noises moved closer. On the stairs now, or so it sounded. Lillian? No. The footsteps were too heavy. A little clumsy—as though he or she were unfamiliar with the layout of the building in the dark. Not good. At the very least, she had a burglar on her hands. At worst, a rapist or murderer. Taking chances would be stupid.

Inspired by the burglar's stumbling, she flipped off the lights in her room. She knew her way around better than any stupid burglar. It might give her just a few seconds' edge.

Decided now—and convincing herself that hovering in the corner in the dark was actually a strategic maneuver instead of an act of cowardice—she held tight to the bat, tucked the flashlight in her pocket and dialed 911 on her cell phone.

"This is Valerie Longstreet at Longstreet Inn and Mystery Theater. I'm reporting an intruder." She reeled off her address softly, rapidly, her heart pounding in her throat.

"We'll send a cruiser around immediately. Please stay on the line until he gets there."

More shuffling, in the hallway now. It was a short hallway, leading right to—

"I can't do that." Valerie squeaked into the receiver. "He's heading toward my door." She dropped the phone into her pocket and braced the bat in clobbering position.

Batter up.

5

FOOTSTEPS, CLEARER NOW, stopped just outside her door. Valerie didn't move a muscle. Except for the trembling ones supporting her knees. And maybe a neurotic little tic in her jaw. A jumpy eyelid. Feeling a little light-headed, she continued to breathe shallowly into the stillness. Kept her breath soft so she could hear and the intruder couldn't...

Another scrape against wooden flooring. When she saw the doorknob, gleaming in the moonlight, shift and turn slightly, she squelched an instinctive squeak. Waited. Backed silently away. She needed swinging room. Nervous, she adjusted her grip on the bat for maximum leverage. The impromptu weapon was probably vibrating with her nerves. *Logistics, Val, think logistics.* She had to. Give room. Door to open—

It did. Quietly.

When a tall, bulky shadow emerged from behind the open door, she shrieked a terrified battle cry and swung the bat.

"Hey—" came a rasping whisper.

Connected. A sickening *thud* of wood meeting hard flesh.

"Oof." The figure doubled over but didn't fall.

She raised the bat again, feeling half nauseous, half victorious, and swung—

"Stop!" A big hand deflected the bat. "*Damn*, that hurts. It's me. *Jack*."

"Oh. God." Dropping the bat to thump and roll across the wooden floor, she clawed through her pocket for her flashlight and turned its shaky beam on— "*Jack?*"

"Turn that damn thing off." Shielding his eyes, Jack made a swipe at the flashlight.

"Sorry." Averting the beam from his face, she reached past him to flip on the lights and studied him anxiously. "Oh, my God. I aimed for your *head*." She was horrified. She could have split it open like a melon. He could be lying on the floor right now, bleeding or worse.

"My *head?*" Jack held his shoulder and glared at her. "I guess it's lucky for me that I'm tall and your aim sucks."

All that adrenaline charging fearfully through her bloodstream cheerfully morphed right into anger. "Well, what did you expect? Sneaking around outside my door like that? You scared the *hell* out of me." She was still shaking with reaction. She'd never actually hit another person like that. With the intent to harm—

"Yeah? Try getting a baseball bat swung at you a couple times. We'll talk nerves then."

Shaken and feeling harassed, she scowled. "Hey, I'm the one being *stalked*, remember? By someone threatening to kill me?"

"I thought you didn't believe that."

"Well, I didn't. I *don't*. But I was feeling alone in this old place, with that spooky serial-killer show on, and I guess I connected that with threatening notes and ghosts and—" She gestured from TV to hallway to ceiling before tossing up her hands in disgust. "Never mind. I just heard noises outside my bedroom door when all the outer doors are supposed to be locked. I should be alone here except for a woman who sleeps like the dead. What did you want me to do? Sound the nonexistent alarms? Rush to investigate? Duh. That always precedes the bloodletting."

"Tell me about it." He carefully rotated his shoulder, then his arm. "Although you did shriek a hell of a loud warning when you swung that bat at me."

"It was sort of a one-woman pep rally before I had to..." She winced and let her words trail off, feeling again the jarring sensation of her bat hitting solid flesh. She'd actually *hit*— "Let me see your shoulder."

"It's fine, damn it." He growled, pulling away.

"Then, *damn it*, why don't you tell me why you broke into my home?"

"Because I—"

The squeal of sirens interrupted whatever he was going to say. He closed his eyes and sighed. "I guess I should be relieved that you at least had the brains to call the cops on your 'intruder' before you decided to play Buffy the burglar basher."

"Well, there is that." When she distantly heard someone pounding on the door, she grimaced and went to confront the police.

"Did you have to tell them I was your boyfriend?"

Somehow, Val hadn't expected those to be the first, shocked words out of Jack's mouth after the cops left. "Why, are you afraid the kids at school will run around chanting *cootie* songs at you?" She gave him an annoyed look. This hot love affair was really getting off to a pathetic fizzle.

"How about neighbor? Concerned friend?"

"Well, gee, Jack, since I don't know what brought you here in the first place, you can't blame me for whatever fiction I come up with. So tell me. Just what the hell *were* you doing sneaking around my inn without permission?"

Jack considered her for a moment, still in a temper, and then his lips twisted. "Actually, I was trying to be discreet."

"Discreet." She gave him a deadpan look. "Gosh, Jack, why wasn't that my first guess?"

He sighed. "I'm serious. I was driving by and thought I saw someone sneak around the corner of your building. I lost him but I thought I should warn you about it."

"Um...telephone? You could call?"

"Didn't have one on me."

"Announce your presence, maybe? Not scare the hell out of me by sneaking around?"

He gave an exasperated sigh. "I knocked and no one answered. I tried the doorbell. Surprise, no answer."

"Busted doorbell and no intercom. I get that."

"So I broke in. You need to change your security codes, by the way—"

"Right, right. So why didn't you speak up once you were inside?"

"Since I never found signs of forced entry, I didn't want to alarm your guests by shouting burglar. I was actually trying to do you a favor."

She grimaced. "I don't have any guests tonight, but, yeah, I see what you mean. Rumors of a burglar wouldn't do anything great for our reputation. Thank you. I think." She thought for a moment, unsure. Something still didn't fit.

"You're alone here tonight?"

Val frowned at that. "I didn't think I was, but I can't see

even Lillian sleeping through police sirens. She must have gone out." Something registered and she looked up at him. "A prowler. You just saw someone sneaking around outside and that was enough for you? That's what made you break in? Isn't that a little too alarmist for a guy like you?"

"Well...not really." He glanced away.

She folded her arms and eyed him with suspicion. "All right, Jack. What aren't you telling me? What's going on?"

He sighed. "No big mystery. It's just that missing necklace of yours. It's been bugging me. I can't help but think it was stolen, and since I'd mostly ruled out you—" He broke off and closed his eyes, obviously cursing a blue streak inside that hard head of his.

She stared, her temper simmering. "Me, *what* exactly?"

He opened his eyes and gave her a level look. "I'll admit I had some vague suspicion...that maybe you faked a robbery."

"Faked a robbery? Of my own necklace?"

"You wouldn't be the first to try it."

"Why on earth would I do something as stupid as that? Do you think I *want* people to believe someone's been robbing me here at the inn? My guests expect this to be a safe place to sleep at night, not a haven for detectives with god complexes or stalkers or burglars and thieves. No innkeeper can afford that kind of reputation."

"An innkeeper might risk it if he was desperate for quick cash. Stash away valuables, say they were stolen, then make a claim against insurers to cover the loss..." Jack's words trailed off and he had the grace to look uncomfortable.

"Insurers? You thought I was guilty of *fraud*? Ethics and legalities aside, again, just how *stupid* do you think I am? Sure, I might get a small sum out of an insurance company, but it wouldn't come close to covering the income I'd miss due to lost business." She glared at him. "That's some high opinion you have of me. Stupid and immoral. To think I actually wanted to *date* you. Of all the nerve."

"But, Val—"

She reached past him and wrenched the door open. "Get out."

"I don't think that's a good idea." Jack was obviously trying to sound reasonable. "You're alone here tonight, in a big old building with a new—but mostly untried—security system. The necklace is still missing, so you could still have a thief on your hands, and then there are the notes, whether you believe in them or not—"

"*Out.*"

"And, damn it, I *did* see someone sneaking around outside. He was trying to get in here."

"Then thank God for my security system, right? Both the electronic one and a *damn* efficient wooden one, if I do say so myself."

Jack absently rubbed his shoulder and started backing out the door. "Fine, then. You have my number. Call if you see or hear anything. I can be over here in five minutes, tops."

"*Goodbye*, Jack."

THE NEXT MORNING, Valerie woke up early, dressed to kill— literally. With Simone gone, she might very well have to stand in for the murderer this weekend and they were going through rehearsals this afternoon. At any rate, dressed in strappy stilettos, a smart little skirt and a fitted navy silk blouse, she felt up to handling the Jack Harrisons of this world.

Thoughtful now, she pawed through her jewelry box, still wishing she could find those sapphires. Maybe the bride would just put them back where they belonged this time.

Except now the little blue cameo was missing, too. She was going to wear it today—sort of an innocent-looking accessory to add just the right twist to a "killer." She sighed and gazed around the room, hoping ghosts had ears. "Eleanor, you cute little bride, you. I really, *really* want those sapphires back."

Getting no immediate response, she grabbed trusty hoop earrings—a girl could never go wrong with simple hoops—and deemed herself ready to face the day. After locking her door, Val trotted down the steps and hurried into the kitchen.

"Morning, Lillian." Valerie smiled when she got a good look at her aunt. Lillian's spectacles, thrust once again into that fluffy helmet of sable hair, listed comically to the left. The dazed expression in her aunt's eyes, as well as the oddly placed glasses, meant Lillian had been up and writing for a while already. "Productive morning?"

"Hmm?" Lillian's vision cleared and she peered at her niece. "Oh, gosh, yes. I woke up hours and hours ago to a clever little idea I just had to pursue. A wonderful morning."

"Well, you missed a bit of drama last night," Val murmured ruefully.

Lillian frowned. "What happened?"

"While you were out— Hey, where'd you go, anyway?"

"Go?" Lillian gave her an odd look and cleared her throat. "I didn't go anywhere. I was here all night. Strange dreams, though. I think I slept too hard. Well, go on. What did I miss?"

"You were here that whole time?" Val frowned. "I can't believe you slept through police sirens."

"*Police sirens?* Oh, my word. Why were they here? What happened? Are you all right? Tell me you weren't hurt."

"I'm fine." Val waved it off. "It was a false alarm. Sort of. Jack thought he saw a prowler on the property, and when he couldn't get my attention, he broke in to warn me. I noticed noise downstairs and called the police."

"Did they find anyone?" Lillian was frowning but not quite at Valerie. No doubt she was filing away details for a future story. The creative mind at work.

"The policemen looked around, but it appears that Jack was the only 'prowler' who managed to break into this place."

"Oh?" Lillian glanced up. "How did that come about?"

Val shrugged uncomfortably. "He was driving by, he said."

Lillian pressed a hand to her heart and seemed to go all dreamy. "So Jack risked life and limb to save you. What a dear. That's about the most romantic thing I've heard of outside of books and the movies. Do *not* let that man go."

"Oh, I have my doubts about the romance *and* the heroism. That man actually believed I—" She waved it off. "Never mind. I don't even want to talk about it. He made me so mad."

"Well. All right." Lillian looked troubled. "I'll drop it for now. Except to suggest that the two of you try to talk out your differences. It sounds to me like he took a huge personal risk following a prowler and then breaking in to warn you. You might think about that a little while you're worrying about whatever quarrel you had." She smiled briefly, then began patting the pockets of her woolen blazer and feeling on her chest where her glasses often dangled from a chain.

Valerie gestured vaguely. "They're on your head."

Lillian frowned then chuckled self-deprecatingly as she plucked the glasses from her hair and perched them on her nose. "I don't know how they end up there, but they often do." She eyed Valerie with approval. "I like that color on you."

Val glanced down at her navy blouse. "Mmm. Me, too. I thought it would be fabulous as a background for that blue cameo you gave me, but—"

Lillian nodded in sympathy. "The bride?" She sighed. "Next time I'll get you a pink one. Or ivory. Subtle beauty. Well, I'd better get back to work before the juices stop flowing." With a wave of farewell, she glided down the hallway.

Weighing Lillian's point about Jack, Val felt a little niggling of guilt. Her aunt was right. Whatever Jack might have suspected of Val, he didn't have to try to sound the alarms on such a personal level when someone was prowling around on her property. He might have been hurt.

She winced. Actually, he *had* been hurt. She'd clobbered him pretty solidly with that bat. Then ordered him off her property.

Damn it. Now she'd have to thank and apologize to a man who'd accused her of fraud and stupidity. *Not* a pleasant way to start a morning.

"YES, MA'AM. NO, REALLY. You've already paid me. I was happy to help." Jack shifted uncomfortably as he listened to his client gush over the phone. Hell, he'd never have taken the missing dog case, anyway, if he hadn't been moved to pity.

Of course, he couldn't swear he had a full load of legitimate cases these days, either. What had happened to all those good old-fashioned divorce cases? Where were the suspicious spouses? Concerned parents? Cynical insurance agents? He knew they were everywhere, but did he get a piece of the action? No, former cop and licensed P.I. that he was, Jack got a little old lady with an absentminded poodle.

But she was a *happy* old lady now, which was kind of nice.

"Well, I'm glad everything worked out." He smiled into the phone. "Just keep identification tags on the dog's collar in case it wanders off again— Right. Okay. Bye, Mrs. Sheridan."

He hung up the phone, sighing in relief as he closed that particular file. He'd just slipped it back in a file drawer when his office door opened and in strode Valerie. Suddenly he was homesick for the dotty poodle. This woman looked irate.

"Morning, Valerie. Can I offer you some coffee?" *To throw in my face?* Hey, why not? A decent second-degree burn would look great with the bruise decorating his shoulder right now.

She rested a hip against his desk, folded her arms and smiled down at him. No, a smart man would never, ever mistake that expression for good humor.

"No coffee? Okay." He cleared his throat.

"I'm here to apologize and say thank you."

"Really. So why do you look bent on violence instead?"

"I'm having a real hard time forgetting all those accusations you threw at me last night."

"Now, Val, I already explained about that."

"Yeah, I heard." She glared at him. "Apparently I'm stupid and immoral enough to stage both stalking notes and theft. Ooh, baby, I *am* the fraud queen. What is with you, anyway?"

"I thought you were here to apologize and offer *gratitude*."

"I changed my mind."

He sighed. "Suppose I apologize first, then."

She stared at him, waiting, measuring.

"I am sorry, Val. I actually—" he tried a crooked half smile "—really *like* you. I have a lot of respect for intelligence and ambition, and you have both. And, sure, those same qualities would have tipped off any other detective that you're not the type to perpetrate fraud."

"Oh." She looked taken aback.

"I'm afraid...I'm not exactly objective where you're concerned. And that's the problem on all kinds of counts."

"I see." She softened her stance and expression, then, sighing, dropped down into a seat across from him. Amazingly, the longer she stared at him, the more her expression relaxed into a rueful smile. "What am I going to do with you, anyway?"

He offered a matter-of-fact solution. "Retain my services?"

"Well, I've been trying to do that for a while, but you keep objecting."

"Not as a brand-new toy for your whodunit crowd to play with—"

She smiled. "My very own boy toy. Sounds like fun."

He groaned.

"Sorry. Continue, please." She wrinkled her forehead into a frown, obviously forcing sobriety.

"Well, when all we had to go on were some notes, I didn't think any immediate action was necessary. They were just notes."

"Right."

"But now add possible theft—"

"But—"

He raised his eyebrows. "Have you found the necklace?"

"Well, no. And in fact—"

"Something else is missing?"

She shrugged. "Just a cameo. It's not horribly expensive, but I wouldn't call it cheap, either. It was brand-new. My aunt gave it to me." She paused. "It's *blue*."

Ghosts again. Jack grimaced. "Fine. Blue or not, it's still missing and possibly stolen, much like your necklace. So take the notes, the possibility of theft and add in the prowler last night…"

Valerie carefully leaned back in her chair, her eyes bright and considering. He'd always suspected a good deal of practical intelligence backed up the hot body, attitude and honeyed looks. She was a beautiful woman. Stunning. Not in an icy, classic way, but warmer, softer. Curvier. She had smooth, creamy skin, and long, golden-brown hair that curved over temple and cheekbone, then fell past her shoulders. Hell, she could have starred in those old spy flicks, with dramatic presence and a well-filled trench coat.

Except for the eyes. A man didn't find calculation or weary sophistication there. She could feign those looks— especially when she lapsed into that vampy, Miss Scarlet act of hers. But for the most part, those warm brown eyes reflected enthusiasm, humor and a lazy sensuality that managed to poke fun at herself—even as it hooked and haunted any male who crossed her path. The woman was dangerous.

"So you think *something* is going on, although maybe you're not sure what it is?" Val asked.

"Exactly. And, as much as I hate to admit it, it would really bug the hell out of me if you got hurt because I didn't do something to prevent it." Great. Nothing like offering your vulnerable back to a woman with too much ammunition already. "You know, since we're neighbors and all. Friends. Sort of." He let his words trail off, feeling increasingly stupid. Juvenile.

She regarded him from beneath lowered lashes, while a curious smile played across those soft lips. "Why, Jack. I think that's the sweetest thing you've ever said to me."

He shook his head but couldn't completely suppress a grin. She seemed to forever provoke that kind of reaction from him. No matter what the circumstances, who was annoyed with whom, what they might have been discussing, *anything*.

"You're easily impressed. I also hate to see dogs playing in traffic. They could get hurt, too."

"Would it kill you to admit you like me just a little?"

"Probably. But we digress."

"Oh, do we?" She laughed. "*We digress?* I've always, always wanted to digress and have someone tell me that's what I was doing." She shook her head and sweetly patronized him. "Jack, you really need to get out more. Normal people don't talk that way. It's so formal. Even highbrow, in a sour old puckered-lips kind of way."

"What I'm trying to say—and I hate this, believe me, I really do—is that I'm willing to act as bodyguard for you. *Briefly*. If you still want my services."

Val leaned forward, eyes sparkling. "Really? My bodyguard?" She raised an eyebrow. "You realize that discretion is still necessary? I don't want it getting out that I need a bodyguard."

"Yes." Really hated this. Already saw it coming.

"So you'd need another reason for hanging around me."

She studied him and he swore he could hear devilish wheels turning in her mind.

"Yes."

She beamed triumphantly and he considered slamming his head in the door. But he'd volunteered for this. Eyes wide open.

"Then the solution is obvious, if hard on your professional P.I. pride. You just charmingly admit to everyone you meet that I wore you down until you finally accepted my generous, long-standing offer. You'll be my hotshot private-eye business consultant. We could even make it a live-in proposition if that suits you best. Naturally, you'd have your own quarters."

The woman knew how to take an opportunity and run with it. Not a surprise, but certainly daunting. "Fine. I'll be your cheesy P.I. temporarily."

"Wonderful! Given the complicated nature of your role, I'll be happy to pay your usual fee—"

"*Oh*, no." Every independent cell of his body rebelled at the idea. "No way will I be under your financial thumb."

She dropped the vamp and seduction act to give him a stern look. "Get real, Jack. You can't afford to do this for free. It's a lot of work and it's bound to interfere with your other cases."

"You want to pay me? Fine. Pay me a finder's fee or something *after* I catch your stalker."

She seemed to weigh the idea. "There's not a lot of profit in that." She eyed him uncertainly. "And none of it guaranteed."

He shrugged. "Sounds like you've got nothing to lose, then."

Her expression grew shrewd. "I'm not so sure about that."

He had to wonder just how many people underestimated Val when she was in her vamp mode. The woman was too smart for his own good. She was absolutely right, whether she knew it or not. Taking this case was a win-win situation for him.

No, he didn't believe he'd be catching Val in the act of fraud, but there was every possibility that the aunt was involved in it. It was just a gut feeling, but he'd bet Lillian was more willing than Val would be to dip into that murky area between right and wrong—if she thought the cause was worthwhile. He was betting that Val and her inn made a sufficiently worthwhile cause from the aunt's perspective.

So, once he had proof, he could turn the aunt in, make some points with the swindled insurance company—a potential future client—and possibly collect a monetary reward. If fraud wasn't an issue, then they were likely dealing with theft, another legitimate case. He'd find the necklace and collect a finder's fee from Val. As for the note writer or stalker, it wouldn't surprise Jack to discover that the notes were somehow connected to the theft or fraud, or even to Val's prowler. "That's my offer, Val. Take it or leave it."

After a moment, she gave a decisive nod. "I'll take it." And smiled. "And rely on your ethics to see me through."

Sharp as a tack. "Fine. Whatever." He sat back in his seat and studied her. "So tell me about your love life."

She curved her lips in a slow, taunting smile. "I've been trying to do just that for weeks now. No luck so far."

He eyed her with strained patience. "We're starting with the notes, Val. Statistically speaking, in most cases the stalker is a former spouse or lover of the victim. The victim in our case, contrarily enough, would be you. God knows you don't look or act like any victim I know. So. Ex-boyfriends, guys you've rejected, one-night stands... Anything?"

She frowned. "I guess I've had my share of relationships, but nothing to inspire death threats."

"Now *that* I find hard to believe." The woman could try the patience of a saint.

"Aww." She grinned unrepentantly. "You're just special."

"That's me. Special as all hell. So just for grins, how about a rundown of your relationships for the past two years."

She feigned horror. "*All* of them?"

"Cut it out, Val." Pen poised, he quietly stared her down. "I'm not buying it."

"What do you mean?"

"The Miss Scarlet act. I didn't get it at first, but I do now."

"Miss Scarlet?"

He sighed impatiently. "You know. Like that board game. The vampy character." He waved off his explanation in favor of his point. "You come on like some hot femme fatale who jumps from guy to guy, but I just don't believe it. You're too ambitious and not shallow enough for that crap. So give. I want names and circumstances."

The look in her eyes was quietly assessing, but the smile didn't waver. "Two whole years' worth?"

"Two years' worth."

She paused, apparently weighing her options.

He just waited.

"Fine." She looked annoyed. "No one."

"*No* one? Pull the other one, lady."

She shrugged. "I've been busy. And picky."

"There's been no one for you. In *two years*."

"No one since California."

He studied her a moment and her gaze didn't waver. "All right. So tell me about California."

"Honestly, Jack. There's not much to tell."

"So it won't take you long, will it? Besides, the suspense is killing me. There's been no one in two years since this stud. I can't wait to hear the details."

Shrugging, she eyed him steadily, one corner of her lips raised in a half smile. "Honestly, Jack. It's such a bland little story that I'd hate to enthrall you unnecessarily."

"Then by all means, tell it to me straight. Otherwise, I'm bound to be fascinated with you by the end of the week."

"You're impossible." She laughed, obviously not offended by his sarcasm. "I swear there really wasn't much to it. I was just involved with a man who was a little overpowering. Socially, I mean. That's why things didn't last."

"He was controlling?"

"Sometimes, though not abusively so. He was charismatic, famous, handsome. I was dazzled, but I also felt... *eclipsed*, I guess you could say. He tended to dominate everyone and everything around him. It wasn't a comfortable feeling, and I felt like my identity was crumbling into tiny little pieces."

"So you broke up with him to retain your identity?" He watched her curiously.

She grinned. "It sounds like an emotionally mature decision, doesn't it? Actually, I might have been pouting and nursing a sprained vanity."

He suppressed a smile. He liked the second scenario better.

"But, seriously, there was no drama to it at all. Looking back, I have to admit it was a pretty shallow relationship.

Breaking up barely caused a ripple in our lives. He moved on to someone else before the week was out, and I had other things to deal with. Like my grandmother's death and settling her estate."

He nodded slowly. "Absolutely no indication that he might still be interested?"

"Not a one. He's not my stalker." She paused, considering him with narrowed eyes. "Tit for tat, Jack. How's your love life been?"

"My love life's not an issue in your case."

"Jack, Jack. Don't be blind, please. We're a tiny bit more than business partners here. So spill it."

"I'm in love with my work."

"How *noble* of you," she said with mock admiration that made him want to smile again. "Have you ever cheated on your work with a woman?"

His amusement fled abruptly. "Yes."

She studied him. "I seem to have phrased that badly."

"Don't worry about it." He cast her an ironic glance. "I might have cheated on work with the woman, but she screwed me over, anyway. Payback's hell."

"Do tell."

"Oh, no." He dug his heels in. "I think I just gave you a hell of a lot more than you gave me."

"If you were in love with your work and then betrayed by a woman...would this have anything to do with why you left the police force?" She raised both eyebrows in sudden enlightenment. "And why your father left?"

He didn't answer.

"Hell, Jack, I think I'm falling into fascination with *you*. That's not at all fair." She gave him a disgruntled look that raised his spirits considerably. "Especially if you won't tell me the rest of it."

"Damn shame, isn't it? Guess we'll have to get back to your case, then."

"I guess we will." She drew out her words, making it clear she was dropping the topic only temporarily. "So you'll be moving in this evening?"

"Yes."

She smiled contentedly. "Then I'll have my detective consultant available…as early as this evening's show?"

He narrowed his eyes, but didn't bother hiding his amusement—or, frankly, his admiration. "Yes. This evening."

The woman never surrendered. She just found a different way to win.

6

HER MIND ON PREPARATIONS for the evening's performance, Val opened the door and smiled in pleased surprise. *"Jack."*

"You were expecting someone else? Actor? Guest? Stalker?"

"Lover?"

He did a double take.

"Well, it seemed so blatantly *missing* from that list you just quoted me." She shrugged, nonchalant. "Come in, then, whoever you are." She was reasonably happy with the classy, Katherine Hepburn-like roll to her *are* and grinned at him.

He shouldered the door open wider and hefted a duffel bag and laptop case past the entrance. "Going for shock value tonight, are we?" he murmured.

"Why not? Right this way." She spoke in a low voice of doom. "And I'll show you to your room."

"Great. Thanks, Elvira."

"Don't mention it." She cast the words and a teasing smile over her shoulder before walking briskly down the hallway. "I hadn't realized how late it was getting. Lots to do still." She gestured toward doors along the way, speaking briskly.

"Lillian's room is on the ground floor at the rear of the building, guests occupy the annex and the second floor, and I'm in the attic. I assume, as my bodyguard, that you'll want an attic room. I put you in the one next to mine." She led him upstairs, turning sharply at the landing to go up another flight.

"And here we are." She stopped at a door beside her own and flipped out a key card. "I think you know how this works."

"Allow me." He accepted the card and unlocked the door.

Valerie stepped back and let Jack enter the room. He tossed his duffel bag on the hardwood floor and looked around. The room was a pleasant combination of earth tones, greens, golden browns, soft beige and hints of burgundy. A simple but sturdy maple dresser and nightstand complemented the antique sleigh bed whose headboard rested against the common wall between their rooms.

He seemed engrossed in that wall as he stared at it for a few moments, before turning back to her. "Nice room. Thanks."

"Sure. You can use the dresser. We'll have to share a bathroom, I'm afraid, and extra blankets are in the—"

"I won't need them."

"All right. About meals. Breakfast won't be a problem, since we offer room service. As for the other times, you can eat with our guests, but only on one condition."

He groaned. "My cheese duties. Right. What are they?"

"*Cheese* duties? Gee, that'll fly well with the guests."

"I promise not to use the term in front of them. Satisfied?"

"We'll see. So. Your duties." She pondered a moment, then smiled. "I think I'll let you use your own judgment. You handled my guests very well the other night."

"Thanks." His voice was wry.

"And there's a dress code. Do you have a suit?"

"Not with me, but, yes," he answered cautiously.

"Good, that will give us a decent fallback if we need it." She put her hands together and rested her chin on the fingertips as she eyed him up and down. "But you, I think, should dress like an eccentric. They'll like that."

"An eccentric?" He watched her warily as she studied him, weighing and picturing different costume possibilities.

"Mmm. Ever smoke a pipe?"

He raised an incredulous eyebrow.

"Okay, forget the pipe. Hats?"

He just stared.

"A cape?"

"You're having too much fun with this," he said.

"No doubt." She cocked her head. "What about blazers? Own any?"

"One."

"Hmm. Wear it on Saturday evenings. The rest of the time…" She paused as she considered him.

"The rest of the time I'll wear what I usually wear."

"Oh, all right." She grinned. "The pipe and hat would have been a lot of fun, though."

"No doubt." He copied her earlier phrase, adding his own inflection.

She laughed. "Breakfast will be outside your door at seven. Lunch is at noon. Dinner at six."

"Fine. My turn."

She raised her eyebrows in question.

"Remember?" He gave her an exasperated look. "I'm not here *just* for your profit and entertainment."

She forced her expression back to a somber line. "Well, of course you're not. So you have questions? Instructions?"

"An explanation first. I carry a gun. I don't like surprises."

"You have a gun? In my *inn?*" She was sincerely appalled.

"I'm a detective and an ex-cop. What do you think?"

"Oh, God."

"You're nervous. Good. Maybe you'll answer my question honestly, then. It's a delicate one, but I wanted you to understand the necessity of it."

"Fine. Honesty. You got it. So what's the question?"

"Are you seeing anyone? Anyone at all?"

"Jack, we already covered this—"

"I mean *anyone*. Casually? Secretly? Openly? Intimately? Are you even mildly involved with anyone at all?"

She tipped her chin up, battling with mild temper. "Well, there was this private detective I met, and I thought things would get hot and heavy really fast with him. But then he got cold feet so I'm left with cold showers." She shrugged, eyeing him with challenge. "Other than that? Nope. No one. I tend to get single-minded with my hopeless crushes. It's more pathetic that way and I can just wallow in all those emotions without distraction."

She raised both eyebrows as though to impart trivia. "You know, unrequited passion is a great well of inspiration to draw on artistically. And I am one of those actor types. If not presently onstage."

He frowned and closed his eyes. "Fine. You're single. If I see a guy other than this detective going into your bedroom, I use force first and ask questions later."

"*Force?*" The notion alarmed her.

"Not actual gunfire unless someone's life is on the line. But force. I would detain him."

"I see," she murmured, a little subdued. "Well, I'd warn the detective, except he hasn't been free with his advances lately."

"Could be he doesn't deem it appropriate now."

"Ah. Business and pleasure?"

"Nasty combination."

"And you'd know."

"I'd know."

"I think I'll need to hear more of this story and soon. I feel at a disadvantage."

"Ah, Val. If anyone's at a disadvantage, it's your pathetic P.I. Have mercy. He's weak."

"Really." She smiled, intrigued. "He could be compromised?"

He just groaned and she laughed.

"Okay, my pathetic P.I. Considering our recent experience, I feel I should warn you about something."

"Around you, I always feel like I'm being tested."

"Truly, it's not all that bad. My part in this weekend's performance is that of victim."

Jack just closed his eyes as though revisiting the sight of Val lying on the floor and "bleeding" from a bullet "wound" to her chest. "As your bodyguard, I think it's my duty to object. Why can't you play the murderer for once?"

"I gave it a shot, but another actor played the role better." She shrugged. "I do good dead people."

"That's reassuring."

"Hey, they say you should always play to your strengths. Mine just happen to be business acumen and dead-body roles."

"So you'll play the dead body and I'll play your dead-body-guard." Jack nodded. "See how I'm being tested? Over and over."

"I know. Poor Jack. That said, though, I should probably start getting ready." Checking her watch, she winced slightly at the time then gave him a quick smile and left, closing the door behind her.

JACK STARED at the closed door, shaking his head. While he stood there, he heard a nearby door open, and then the sound of feminine humming drifted through the wall. A drawer opened and closed, the floor creaked and he heard the faucet running. A few moments later, the shower.

So, as though he weren't already shaking hands with insanity, he'd have to endure the sounds of Valerie, naked with only a wall separating them. No doubt she'd noisily enjoy all kinds of sensual pleasures while he paced the confines of his torture chamber.

Tested. He was being tested.

After a brief, very cold shower of his own, Jack dressed in khakis and a nice shirt, and sought out the dining room. It was showtime. Nodding pleasantly to the half-dozen new faces around the table, he glanced inquiringly at Valerie, who came to stand next to him.

"Everyone, I have an unadvertised treat for you this weekend. We have a genuine private detective here to help us with our investigations. This is Jack Harrison, who owns a detective agency just down the street. He's not going to solve the case for you unless we stump you, but he is available for questions and suggestions. Jack?"

Caught off guard, Jack just stared for a moment, until her smile grew pointed. He turned his gaze on the group, offered another general nod, then turned back to Valerie.

She waited patiently, but for what exactly...hell, he didn't have a clue. He wasn't a performer. What did she expect?

Her expression grew strained. "Maybe you'd like to give us some *pointers* for investigating murders?"

"Oh. Sure. Leave the homicides for the police to solve."

Mistaking his very serious response for a joke, several of the guests laughed.

Valerie's lids lowered, though her smile never wavered. "I'm sure he'd be willing to answer more specific questions later if you'd like to approach him individually."

Jack considered her. The woman was unstoppable. That deserved a little credit. "Sure."

Valerie nodded then turned to help an older woman serve the meal. While she did so, a younger, sweet-faced woman wearing a discreet uniform tapped Valerie on the shoulder and whispered into her ear. Valerie nodded and spoke in a low but not inaudible voice. "You can start in the sitting room and work your way around the lower floor from there." The woman nodded, her smile nervous, then turned to leave.

Jack watched curiously. Strange that a maid would interrupt a meal to ask where to clean first. But what did he know about running a small inn?

When Valerie returned to the kitchen, an older woman turned inquisitive gray eyes on Jack. "So you're joining us this weekend. How fascinating. Isn't that fascinating, Harry?" She turned to a sleepy-eyed gentleman to her right.

"*Fascinating*, dear." If the man were any more *fascinated*, he'd be facedown, snoring in his shrimp scampi.

A twenty-something man sitting next to a woman Jack presumed to be his twenty-something wife, spoke across the table to Jack. "This is our first-ever mystery weekend. I didn't know we'd have a real-live detective, too."

Beats having a dead one, Jack supposed. He nodded politely then turned back to his dinner. What was taking Valerie so long?

"Oh, we've heard so much about this place from some neighbors of ours. So we had to give it a try ourselves. Miss Longstreet apparently goes all out for these dos." This from the young woman, her eyes eager yet nervous.

Jack gave her a curious look. "All out?"

"But I guess that's no surprise." Her eyes shone with even greater enthusiasm. "I heard Valerie at one time wanted to be an actress herself. I bet that's a good story." Her words drew nods around the table.

"Think so?" Jack set his fork down and, feeling only minor guilt, glanced around the table for more information.

"Yes, indeed," responded a woman sitting next to the young couple. "I heard she played a bit part on a television drama before she inherited this building and moved home for good."

An actress on television. He'd have to file that away for future reference. Meanwhile, he did have a job to do.

Jack cleared his throat and then nodded to the woman who'd offered the information about Valerie's acting ambitions. "So you've attended these mysteries before? How many, if you don't mind my asking?" He infused his words with harmless curiosity.

"Two matinees and one dinner mystery. I loved all of them."

Jack made polite noises. "What about everyone else? Any other repeaters?"

An older gentleman, quieter than the rest and obviously alone for the weekend, gestured with almost embarrassed enthusiasm. "Me."

Jack nodded pleasantly. "You've been here before?"

"Almost every month. I love Ms. Longstreet's matinees."

"So you attend all the new shows?"

"Oh, no. Just the matinees." The older man, whose name tag declared him to be Mr. Thomas, cleared his throat. "This is my first weekend mystery. I've been looking forward to this. I just love puzzles, and whodunits are the best kind of puzzle." Nods around the table signified agreement. "And Valerie's new cook is very accomplished." A mild frown came and went, and the man discreetly patted his midsection. "Better than the old one."

After dessert, the group took their after-dinner drinks into the library, a custom at Longstreet Inn, one of the repeaters explained to Jack. Valerie had just rejoined the group and was seeing to individual needs when a scream sounded from another room. It ended abruptly.

An unholy smile crossed Mr. Thomas's lips, and he leaped to his feet to race out the door. Jack was impressed as all hell with the man's agility. Untold depths there. An assortment of yelps and exclamations followed as the group bustled off in Mr. Thomas's wake.

Jack exchanged a glance with Valerie, who observed her guests with a satisfied smile. "Has there been a murder?" he asked facetiously after the room had cleared.

"Your cue, Detective." She turned the smile, now nearly as gleeful as Mr. Thomas's, on Jack. He grimaced slightly, but left to follow the fresh exclamations and excited chatter.

He stopped in front of an open door. Like all the rooms on the lower level, this room had an elaborately carved sign posted outside of it. This particular sign indicated he was entering the garden room. He entered and discovered the group gathered in a circle around the nervous maid, who lay on the floor in a dramatic pose. Virtually canopied by greenery, she looked pale and still and there was broken pottery on the floor next to her.

Mr. Thomas turned a huge grin on Jack, then tried, obviously, to contain his enthusiasm to a more dignified level. "The investigation begins."

"SO WHAT DO YOU THINK SO FAR?" Valerie sat with Jack on a couch in her office later that evening, a glass of wine in her hand as she eyed him curiously. They were taking a break from the evening, while the guests were supposed to be mulling their evidence over drinks and desserts.

"Interesting way to spend a weekend." Jack gazed thoughtfully into his own glass of wine. "But I thought you were going to be the victim."

"Oh, I will be. We like multiples on the weekend, just for a change of pace. We can't do it all the time, though, since it requires more bodies to fill roles."

He winced. "So to speak."

She grinned.

"So is it like this all weekend? Socializing, asking questions, waiting for bodies to turn up?"

"Well, we have until Sunday morning to drop all the clues and allow guests a chance to solve the case. We break at certain times for meals, snacks, teatime or drinks, and there are certain times when guests can question suspects in the case."

"And you do this every month, in addition to your dinner shows and matinees?" Jack gazed at her with fresh respect.

"Every month. As for the stories themselves, we showcase a new one every three months for the weekend productions. Matinee and dinner productions we rotate every few weeks. Aunt Lillian would die of overwork otherwise, though she is pretty prolific."

"Has Lillian ever been published?" Jack sipped at his wine.

"Short stories here and there. We sort of cooked up this mystery dinner theater idea together. She doesn't much like the business end of things, but she's a great writer. We work well together. She's friend, partner and family."

Jack nodded thoughtfully. "So where are your parents?"

"They died in a car accident when I was twelve."

He frowned. "I'm sorry. I didn't know."

She nodded. "My grandmother raised me."

"The grandmother who left you this place?" He glanced around her office.

She smiled. "Yes."

"What about your aunt?" His attention sharpened for a moment. "Wouldn't she have inherited?" *A motive…?*

"Paternal grandmother and Lillian was my mother's sister. They're not related except through marriage."

"Ah." He nodded. *Motive nonexistent.* "So tell me about your parents."

"My mom was amazing. Beautiful, talented." Valerie smiled. "She was a model and actress, just hitting her stride when she was killed. She'd had her first movie deal and was hopeful of another. Dad thought he had it clinched for her."

"Your dad did?"

"He was her manager. They tended to mix business and pleasure on a regular basis."

"I see." Val was nothing if not persistent with her points.

"It made for an interesting childhood, anyway. I spent some time in California living with my folks, and a lot of time here when their work lives got in the way."

"Did it bother you? That their work lives got in the way?"

"I was a kid. Of course it bothered me. I understood, but

it bothered me." She grinned. "I was a quiet little bookworm at heart, but it didn't take long for me to realize that a kid had to make a lot of noise to be heard in a family like mine."

"Makes sense."

She shrugged and took a sip of her wine.

"Are you still a bookworm?"

She looked startled and thought a moment. "I suppose. I'm a lot busier now than I was as a kid."

"Interesting." No, revealing. Stunning. First a bookworm and now a fake vamp. The woman was inherently reserved. Val, an introvert? Even *shy*? He'd suspected there was more to her than the Miss Scarlet act she put on, but this? It was a complete role reversal in his mind. So to speak. *Role reversal*. That would be Val's influence.

She studied him for a frowning moment, then tipped her chin up and grinned. "'Interesting'? Jack, you sound like a shrink. 'Aaaaah. Eenterrestink. I sink Herr Freud vould say yur noodle es tweested in tiny leetle knots.'"

He chuckled.

"Oh, my God. You laughed. Just came right out and did it. Did it hurt?"

"Smart-ass."

"I'm serious. You have a wonderful laugh. Why are you so miserable that I've never heard it before?"

He gave her a shaming look. "Because I'm working, remember? And my latest client is tying me up in *tweested leetle knots*."

She goggled, her glass tipping precariously as her wrist went slack. "And a joke. You even told a *joke*."

He rolled his eyes but wanted to laugh again. Val's exaggerated shock was entertaining, even if it came at his own expense.

"Jack, I'm so touched. I got to share this moment with you. We'll be close forever and ever now."

He tried to look stern. "I think I agree with Herr Freud."

"Sure, I'm nuts. Whatever. It's all relative, anyway."

"Relative—?"

Lillian whisked into the room. "Val, darling. You're on!"

"Oh!" Val ditched her glass and flashed Jack an irrepressible grin. "Don't mind me. I need to go be murdered."

As Val left the room, Jack just shook his head and stood up. Ten minutes later, he heard his cue. A sharp feminine scream, a crash and deathly silence.

Hearing a rush of footsteps in that direction—and actually immune to the grisly noises of "death" this time—Jack took a deep breath and waited for the excited crowd to settle. Then he walked down the short hallway toward the noise and entered the room, looking as suave and intellectually mysterious as possible. He nodded at the avid faces around him, then turned to inspect the scene.

"So we have a murder." He kept his voice bland, as though he could be smoking a pipe and contemplating the philosophies of life. He was performing for Valerie's sake. A trained little monkey, apparently. Call him infatuated.

Hmm. Maybe he could tease the little pretender into betraying herself with another grin. That would make his night.

Mr. Thomas spoke up from the chair on which he lounged. "So it would seem. But not all things are as they seem." He nodded wisely, puffing theatrically on a real pipe.

Jack suppressed the urge to scratch his nose and nodded briefly. "Very true. So, let's compile our observations." Jack looked around the room. "Details. What's important here?"

"Two glasses on the table. Both half-empty." A middle-aged woman smiled delightedly as she spoke up.

"Yes. What do we deduce from that?" *Deduce.* An excellent word. Pompous, Sherlock Holmes-ish. He watched Val's lips. She should like that one almost as much as *digress*.

"There were two people in the room," the woman announced triumphantly.

"Correct." Jack dipped his head. "We also theorize that this other person may or may not be the killer, and that the woman probably knew this person." He glanced briefly at the "corpse" lying on the floor and tried not to grin. She was squirming. Imperceptibly, really, except he knew where to look.

Speculation continued, with guests picking out one suspect after another and debating motive and opportunity. As expected, analysis eventually drifted to the victim's supposed lover.

At this point Mr. Thomas apparently felt compelled to speak up. "The lover. A crime of passion. That, of course, begs the question of whether she *deserved* to die."

Jack's attention sharpened. He didn't particularly like this line of thought, considering Valerie was the murder victim currently under discussion. "An investigator's job is not to weigh moral justification but to find and interpret evidence that could be admitted in a court of law."

"I'm sure you're right." The man puffed. "But sometimes I think we neglect the more important truths when we ignore justification. Some reprehensible acts *are* justifiable."

"But those are exceptions, not the rule." Jack gave him a hard look then forced a smile. "I believe we've collected as much evidence as we're going to find here, so let's take this discussion to the war room. Any objections or additions?" He glanced around. Several head shakes responded to his question, and he gestured to the doorway.

Everyone left except Mr. Thomas, who continued to sit and puff and ponder. He stared, unfocused, at Valerie's "body" lying on the floor.

Unnerved by that look, Jack spoke up. "Mr. Thomas? It's time to leave the scene now. So the staff can clean up the room."

"Of course. I'm sure cleanup is the hardest part." Slowly, Mr. Thomas got to his feet, stared a moment at Jack, then turned to go. After he left the room, Jack smiled at those who lingered in the hallway. "I'll join you all in a moment."

He closed the door and turned back to Valerie, who was sitting up and rubbing the hip on which she'd been resting.

"What do you know about him?"

"Mr. Thomas?"

"Yeah, Mr. Thomas. You really have some sick people for guests. Did you hear his theory? The answer to the whodunit is that the victim *deserved* to die? Lock your door tonight."

"Mr. Thomas does get melodramatic during investigations, doesn't he? Just so you know, the man's retired, and he loves to ponder and spout philosophy whenever he sees an opening. Otherwise, he's just adorable. Seriously. He has an almost touching enthusiasm for mysteries and quilting."

"Quilting, huh? What does he use for material? Body parts?"

A peal of surprised laughter escaped. "Spooked you, did he? What happened to our hardened cop and cynical P.I.?"

"Hey, when 'adorable' little old men talk about justifiable homicides, it's enough to curdle even cold blood."

"Honestly, Jack, I swear he's harmless. He just likes the spotlight every once in a while—loves to be the one who solves the crimes. I think he's bored."

"I think he bears looking into."

She rolled her eyes and continued in a mockingly soothing voice. "Now, Jack. The man's eligible for our senior citizen discount. Even if he's writing the letters, I don't think I have anything to fear from him. Remember my wooden security system? It even takes out the professionals, you know."

He narrowed his eyes, but before he could respond, a knock sounded at the door. It opened and Mr. Thomas ducked his head in, his eyes dancing with excitement. Jack just stared, surprised by the change in the older man. Good grief, it was like Jekyll and Hyde. Here was Val's adorable older man—the same excited, if shy man he'd met at dinner tonight. He could even picture the man cheerfully gossiping and plying a careful needle.

Mr. Thomas was waving an envelope at them. "I found this note on a table in the war room—but it's addressed to Valerie. Maybe it's a clue?"

Jack and Val stared at the envelope in Mr. Thomas's hand. It was made of a familiar parchment-colored paper. Sure, it was a clue, but not to any murder mystery Val produced. She and Jack exchanged a glance before Val responded to Mr. Thomas.

"I think it's a personal message. For me."

7

"So we have a sneaky coward of a stalker." Val scowled at the note. This idiot was interfering with business now. One mystery bumping into another just didn't make for smooth flow.

Jack nodded. "Certainly one with the ability to smuggle a note into the library in the middle of one of your shows."

Lillian grimaced. "Well, there were a lot of people coming and going this afternoon. Cleaning people, extras for the show—multiple bodies, you know—plus guests, food delivery people, restaurant staff."

Jack nodded. "We have a date now, though, which is new."

The note itself had turned out to be a small calendar of the month of October, clipped from what looked like a women's magazine. The square representing day two was circled in blue marker. A handful of words had been snipped and glued onto the square: Val's Special Day. Funeral at 7 p.m.

"Well, hey, at least my death is special. I feel much better now. My very own day to die. I'm so touched."

"Val." Lillian sounded scandalized.

"What? Should I go cry into my pillow? Forget that. I'm sick of threats."

"Are you scared?" Lillian looked alarmed now.

"*No*, damn it, I'm frustrated and I'm really starting to get pissed. This 'stalker' is interfering with business now. I want him stopped. Hell, doesn't this amount to harassment? At least?" She gave Jack a challenging look. "Well, sitting back and ignoring the attention hound isn't getting me anywhere. Maybe I should retaliate. A little harassment to pay back a little harassment? That's sounding pretty good right now."

"Val, take it easy—" Jack tried to soothe, while Lillian looked thoughtful.

"*No*. I'm through taking it easy. So this guy thinks there's going to be a *party*, does he? On October 2." Val smiled with hostile enthusiasm. "Fine. I'll throw this shindig *myself*."

"Val—"

"Invitations have to go out immediately. But there *will* be a party on October 2. We're all going to dance on my grave."

Jack rubbed at his temple as though to ease a sudden pang there. "I'll admit that bravado can be a really constructive force. But you might be going a little overboard here."

"Give it up, Jack. I'm throwing the party." She gave him a narrow-eyed look. "I'd think any self-respecting P.I. would be celebrating, too. I'm going to invite everyone I can think of—including your entire suspect list. Maybe we'll even annoy this guy into stupid action so we can nail him once and for all."

"I can see some merit in that, sure, but—"

"Great. Invitations will go out Monday. Tuesday at the latest. But first, I think…I *really* think we need a theme for this party. We're going to make a big splash. Yes, that would please the hell out of me." She turned to her aunt. "So? Any brainstorms?"

Lillian looked startled, and then mildly intrigued. "Go as your favorite murder victim?" She offered the suggestion hesitantly. "It's a little over the top, I suppose, but it works for the theme of the inn. And, apparently, your mood." She smiled ruefully at her niece.

Val gasped. "*Lillian*. That's utterly brilliant." She gave her aunt an exuberant hug, as ideas raced and coalesced. "We'll call it a Come as You Died party. *Yes*. I love it."

"We could leave theatrical makeup and props at guests' disposal." Lillian was thinking, rapidly. "Maybe offer the services of staff members for costume and makeup application?"

"Excellent idea. I could ask some of our contract help to pitch in, too." Val smiled wickedly. "Do you know how much fun it's going to be to decorate this place for it? Token clues planted everywhere. Abandoned weapons, smudged glass, spatters of fake blood, curtains and carpet askew…"

Lillian chuckled. "I do love your twisted mind, dear. You must get that from my side of the family."

Val grinned at her, in complete accord.

"Yeah. You're both nuts." Jack groaned. "And complicating my job, damn it. Hell, I can see it already. The guy turns out to be a true-blue psycho—pun intended—and I'll have the pleasure of finding your gun-shot body all over again—"

"No, not *gun-shot*." Val tapped a fingernail on her chin. "Stabbed, I think. It's so much more dramatic. More personal. You know, I would just hate to be shot and killed. That would mean the killer didn't even care enough to get his hands dirty getting rid of me. I'd like someone to at least expend some time and energy on my death. Wouldn't you?"

"God, that's twisted." Jack shook his head and laughed. "You and your sicko mind will be the death of me yet."

"Hey, that's a great idea." Valerie gave him an intrigued look. "We could come to the party as a murder-suicide."

Jack stared. "I think I fear for your stalker."

"That's the spirit. We'll beat him yet."

While Val and Lillian discussed party preparations, Jack weighed possibilities. He hadn't thoroughly researched Lillian's background yet, but so far she seemed as clean and straightforward as Val. No outstanding debt and no criminal record—which cast insurance fraud into serious doubt in his own mind. Still, if Lillian was desperate on behalf of her niece... Jack studied Val. But he'd seen the bank records. Val *wasn't* desperate, so there was no need for her aunt to be.

Hell, the aunt even taught writing classes at a local community college for a pathetic little salary. It couldn't possibly compensate for the time she put into the job. So, apparently, the woman wasn't mercenary and, he had to conclude, she probably wasn't stealing from her niece, either. Maybe someone else was stealing the jewelry? He'd look into it.

As for the notes...would one of Lillian's writing students pull a stunt like that? To impress his teacher? Lillian was just eccentric enough and downright lovable enough...yeah, he could see it. An idiot kid might go to a whole lot of trouble to impress her.

Still, for the guy to actually name a *date*... That was going too far. Yeah, it'd be a good idea to keep a closer eye on Val. Just in case.

After Lillian bustled off to set plans in motion, Val turned to Jack with an expectant smile. "You know what? This is going to be a *great* party. Even if nothing comes of stalker boy, it'll be great publicity for both of us. Promo for the inn, networking and promo for you."

"Still, this party—a Come as You *Died* party? Set on the day of your supposed funeral? You realize that you're publicly laughing at this guy's threats. Not to mention stealing his thunder. You're bound to piss him off royally."

She gave Jack a calculating little smile. "Good. Isn't that exactly what we want? An angry stalker? One who's too emotional to think straight? He'll make mistakes, then, right?"

"Sure, he might." Jack gave her an exasperated look. "He might also work up the nerve to actually *kill* you before I can stop him. Or beat him to the punch."

Monday morning, Val was still thinking about Jack's reaction to her party idea. *Alarmist.* Well, she had every right to call the stalker's bluff if she wanted. It was, after all, *her* business the lunatic was disrupting. She wondered who could be doing this. More and more, though, she had to doubt the adolescent theory. It would be hard for a kid to find his way into the inn without drawing notice. Maybe a college kid—

College kid? Lillian's creative writing class. Now there was a thought. She'd have to mention it to Jack.

A knock at the door interrupted her musings and she glanced up. "Come in."

The door opened and in walked one of the last people she'd expected to see in her office again. "Simone."

"The black sheep returns. Can I come in?"

"Sure." Rallying, Val stood up and rounded her desk to close the door after Simone.

The actress seemed oddly amiable. Almost nervous, too, which was saying something, given that the woman moved with the canny grace of a cat most of the time.

"What can I do for you?" Val kept her tone light and sat behind her desk.

Simone slid into a chair directly across from her. "I'm here to apologize for the last time I was in your office. I was rude and unprofessional. You should have fired me on the spot."

Valerie studied her a moment. "You seemed to believe what you were saying at the time, though."

"Maybe I *wanted* to believe everything I was saying at the time. I was jealous and unhappy."

Valerie nodded.

"I've just been under a lot of pressure. Self-imposed, mostly." Simone shrugged. "I believe I should be further along in my acting career by now, be rising higher than…" She waved her hands around obliquely, her expression apologetic.

"You feel you should be doing something more ambitious than acting in a mystery dinner theater?" Valerie clarified.

"*Yes*. I mean, I'm sure this is very *nice* for a theater of this type, but it's not what I visualized for myself. I'm not sure you can understand…"

"Oh, you might be surprised." Valerie smiled a little.

"Anyway. I'd like my job back. If it's still open." When Val didn't immediately reply, Simone explained in a flat tone. "My rent is due and I didn't get a part I auditioned for. You could say I'm a little desperate."

Ah. "It's true the position's still open, but how do I know you won't leave me in the lurch again?"

"I don't think my options are any thicker on the ground than yours are." Simone gave her an arch look.

Val raised an eyebrow. "Well, gee, since you groveled so nicely."

"I didn't think you were the type to require groveling."

"From employees? No. I do, however, expect some changes."

"Like?" Simone looked wary.

Val let some of her impatience show. "Like you should try learning your lines. Showing up on time. Showing up at *all*. Why should I give you this chance if you can't fulfill the most basic of your obligations?"

Simone nodded. "That's fair enough."

"And your attitude—"

"Right. I'll be good. Little worker bee, that's me."

Val eyed her suspiciously for a moment. "All right."

"Really? I get it back?"

"Yes. But I will be watching you."

"I understand." Simone smiled. "Thank you, Miranda."

Valerie stiffened in surprise. "Miranda?" That was the name of a character she'd once played—

Simone shrugged, bored and breezy now that she'd gotten what she wanted. "I used to watch that soap every day. You weren't too bad. You did okay with the mushy parts and the funny parts. Even the bad-girl lines."

"But?"

"The melodrama. You needed to work it more. And the waterworks? Not convincing at *all*."

Val frowned. "I didn't think anyone would remember me in that role. But you weren't the only one to comment on that part of it. I never could learn to cry on command. Not convincingly."

"Oh, I can." Simone sighed in pleasure. "One of my stronger talents. It just astounded my coaches and even the occasional producer. Really. You should create a crying part for me here. I can weep at the drop of a hat, and I don't get puffy or red in the face. I can even do it without smudging makeup or flattening my hair." She touched a lock of the gleaming mass. It was shorter today. More layers in front, artfully framing Simone's stunning features.

"Tears, huh? Let me talk to Lillian and see what she can come up with."

After Simone left, Valerie stared into space for a moment, recalling a more carefree time in her life. She'd actually taken a lot of pride in her short stint on that soap opera before her grandmother's death. Not that she'd trade what she had now for the past, but it might have been fun to see where that other path would have taken her.

So, sure, she could sympathize with Simone. But she had her limits. Should the woman glance twice at Jack now, for example, Valerie just might have to resort to violence. Especially since Jack was calling a hands-off himself. A woman could endure only so much frustration before snapping.

"A soap-opera queen. Wonders never cease."

Val jumped, caught sight of Jack in the open doorway and glared. "Don't *do* that."

"Sorry. Didn't mean to scare you."

She nodded but didn't lower her guard. "So how long were you eavesdropping on us?"

"Long enough to hear a few tantalizing hints about your glamorous past."

"Not so glamorous. I was more soap-opera *pawn* than soap-opera queen. Not the producer's favorite."

"Really. Did you play the good girl or the bad girl?"

"So cynical." She had to smile. "It was much more complicated than that. I was a good girl whom life had treated terribly so I acted like a bad girl. Fascinating?"

"In an involved sort of way, yes. So what happened?"

She sighed dramatically. "The audience never fell in love with me. My co-star was tons more charismatic than I could ever hope to be. So they ended up killing me off. It was tragic."

"And the co-star? Did they kill her off, too?"

"Him. My on-screen and sometimes *off*screen boyfriend. Nope, they kept him and even reincarnated my old role with a different actress. You see, they never found the body." She gave him a wise look. "Cardinal soap rule. Unless there's a deathbed scene and a body, these characters just don't stay dead."

"So your character lives through another actress now. And the boyfriend? Who is he and what's he doing these days?"

"He's still with the soap, last I heard. Ray Guzmano."

Jack looked intrigued. "He's even done some movies."

"See? Charisma."

"And he was your boyfriend in real life, too. The guy in California, right? The one who eclipsed you. That was him?"

"Yes." She grinned. "But as I said before, it was a very brief, shallow thing between us. I was too fickle to enjoy being upstaged even on our dates." She lowered her voice confidingly. "He had better hair than mine, too, and that was *un*forgivable."

Jack looked amused. "I see. And he's not pining after you, either?"

"Not according to the tabloids. He has women hanging all over him. Girlfriends, groupies, crazed fans, you name it."

Jack nodded thoughtfully, then glanced down the hallway where Simone had disappeared. "So what was the deal with Simone? Why'd she come back?"

Val peered at him through her lashes and smiled. "Oh, Simone came back for *you*, handsome."

Jack gave her an exasperated look.

Sighing in disappointment—a girl should have a legal right to prod and poke at Jack's type of guy—Val dropped the vampy act. "It seems she came back for the paycheck. She didn't get a role she wanted, but the bills must still be paid. Not that I think she'll stay very long."

"You think that's all there is to it?"

Val shrugged. "Who knows what's going on in her head beyond cash."

"Cash can make people do a lot of things."

"Maybe so. Whatever. Simone's a decent enough actress that I can't always tell when she's being genuine. But it looks like I have my murderess back in time for our next performance and, frankly, I'm too grateful to question it right now."

"Maybe that's just it. Maybe you should question it. Or maybe I should," he murmured thoughtfully, almost to himself.

"That works." Already thinking ahead to the next production, Val turned back to her desk. "*You* think about stalkers while I contemplate murder. Thank God Simone came back and thank God she was still here when we started rehearsing this story line. Now I don't have to be the knife wielder."

"You would have been the murderer next? I'm sorry I'm going to miss that."

"That was the original plan. I was going to fill in until

we trained Mandy for the part. She'd do it next week. Now that Simone's back, all I have to worry about is whether she learned her lines this time."

"An actress who doesn't learn her lines or even show up half the time? Why do you bother? Why do you work with someone like that? Actors and actresses can't be too hard to come by. This looks like entertaining work and, knowing you, the pay's probably fair. Can't you find someone more reliable?"

"Well, sure, but—" She made a face.

"Go on."

"It's just that I've been there. Where Simone is. Unsettled, torn. So I can identify. It's hard not to lash out when you're pulled in two different directions—a *should* and a *want-to*—and they keep getting confused."

"I don't understand."

"You probably wouldn't unless you'd been there yourself. As an actor part of you wants to reach for that brass ring because ambition says you *should* want it. The other part is tempted to try this other, less stellar thing because it could be fun. Then, the ambitious side makes you feel guilty for settling for the other thing, and then the practical side makes you feel guilty for feeling guilty."

He watched her for a moment, and she could almost picture him trying to rearrange her explanation into something that made sense in his logical mind. "Sounds like a vicious tangle."

"That it is. It can drive you nuts if you let it."

"Hence your patience for Simone's moods."

"Hence." She grinned. "Gosh, but you're a smart detective."

As the "funeral" date approached, Val focused most of her energy on performances and preparing for the upcoming festivities. Jack, former cop and current cynic, was following through on his precautionary urges. He'd turned into an expressionless shadow who dogged her heels, pawed through her mail and kept his professional cool every moment of the day.

Talk about annoying. It wasn't so much that she disliked the idea of a hot detective following her around. She just wished *he* thought it was something to smile and drool about.

She smiled, feeling an evil urge to misbehave. Maybe it was time to give the detective something to drool about.

She found him in the gold sitting room, going through a stack of files that looked way too familiar by now. Staff files. He was studying them again—as though he might have overlooked something during the last dozen times he'd pored over them.

"Jack." She spoke in a weak, quavery voice, discreetly brandishing an envelope she'd snagged from her desk.

He glanced up immediately, eyes sharp, then concerned as he focused on the paper in her hands. "Val? What's wrong?"

"Nothing." She made it sound like more than nothing. Who the hell said she couldn't act? "It's just..."

"Yes?"

She tried for hesitant. Strove for Simone's shifting gaze, Mandy's innocence and her own subtle provocation. "Could we go to my office?"

Jack rose immediately and followed her down the hall into her office, where she shut the door behind him and pounced.

He caught her reflexively, his grip hard, while she sought his mouth with hers, sinking deep and sighing. His hold softened. "I thought something was wrong," he murmured against her lips.

"Something is wrong." She slid her lips down his chin, biting at his jawline before nipping her way down his neck. "You've been avoiding my company."

"I've hardly left Longstreet Inn in the past week, and I've kept so close an eye on you that it's driving you nuts."

"Men are so literal." She groaned against his neck. "I'm talking exclusive company. You and me alone together."

"The envelope..." he whispered, his voice raspy. She tugged at his earlobe with her teeth.

"Just my grocery list. Sue me."

"That's low."

"Yeah. Unconscionable. So shut up and kiss me."

"You've been driving me crazy." His hold on her tightened until he'd lifted her completely off her feet. He dragged her mouth to his for a hungry, soul-deep kiss.

Val returned it feverishly, her hands restlessly tugging at his shirt, his pants, buttons, belt. When he started yanking on her clothing, she laughed in weak relief. "Finally."

When the door supporting Jack's back shook beneath pounding, they both jumped and stared at each other. Valerie wanted to weep in frustration. "No. It's locked. Ignore it," she whispered. "It'll go away."

"Val. Maybe this wasn't such a good—"

She kissed him again, persisting until his hold on her tightened and his breathing grew ragged.

More pounding. And more insistently.

"*Valerie Longstreet.* I know you're in there." A woman's voice. Vaguely familiar.

Valerie groaned and pulled back while Jack stepped away from the door. "Damn. Damndamn*damn*." She stared at the door, trying to focus. "I can't believe— She'd stop by *now*, of all times? Aaaargh." She turned back to Jack, who looked equally hot and frustrated. *"Don't leave*, okay? We're not through and I'll be right back. Not a finger. Not a toe. Not an inch. *Please.*"

He dropped onto the couch and closed his eyes.

More pounding. "Hey. What kind of an establishment is this, anyway? Open this door immediately."

After quickly smoothing her blouse and glancing furtively into a wall mirror at her tousled reflection, Valerie opened the door with a smile so brazen she surprised even herself. "Mrs. Burlington! Just the woman I've been *dying* to see. Tell me you're here to review Longstreet Inn. *Finally*. You'll put us on the map, won't you?"

"What? But I—" She tried to peer past Valerie.

"Oh, no." Valerie grinned and shooed Mrs. Burlington back while she closed the door behind them. "No backstage peeks until you've seen the real performance. I don't want to spoil the mystery before you've seen the mystery." She was mildly impressed with her own off-the-cuff lines. "So why don't we backtrack to the foyer and give you the full treatment."

"Wait just one moment. Valerie Longstreet, I will not be shoved aside or dodged. There was someone in there with you."

"Huh?"

Mrs. Burlington glared—a disturbing expression, given the brazen pink lipstick she'd smeared on her lips to match her suit. Val supposed her own lipstick was kissed off, if not smeared worse than Mrs. Burlington's.

"You have a man in there, Valerie. I heard voices." Her bust was heaving with outrage. "And noises. I heard *noises*." She raised her eyebrows, implying the noises had been anything but innocent.

Ignoring the implications, Val tried for careless disregard. "Oh. Well, it *is* my office. I conduct business in there. We hold the mystery performances on the rest of the first floor. I'm sure you'd be more interested in touring that than in hearing about the loads of paper goods I need to order." She smiled.

"What I heard didn't sound like business. It sounded like—like—" She flustered, fumbled, then widened her eyes. "Like kissing. And *sex*."

"Mrs. Burlington!" Valerie was shocked. Entertained as hell, sure—now that her frustrated blood had cooled enough that she could appreciate the situation—but *shocked*. She'd never before heard the word *sex* spoken with such outraged zest. The worst of it was, Val was missing out on all of that shocking sex, thanks to Mrs. Burlington's interruption. Maybe the woman should give up on her restaurant reviews and concentrate solely on the gossip she enjoyed so damn much.

By the time Val managed to cajole and argue Mrs. Burlington into Lillian's tender keeping, it was nearly an hour later. Mrs. Burlington seemed intent on waiting out Val's office guest—fodder for a gossip article masquerading as another scathing review, no doubt. But they were both doomed to disappointment.

When Val returned to her office, she discovered the door open and the room empty. Her detective had flown the coop. Well, she *had* been gone an entire hour, for heaven's sake.

Trying to be reasonable, Val set out to look for Jack to see how far he'd run—and not just in the literal sense.

She discovered him and her answer in the gold sitting room.

"Hi." She spoke quietly.

He glanced up from the files he'd reclaimed. "Hi."

"You moved."

"You took a long time."

She nodded.

"And, to be honest, I thought we should hold off. At least for a while."

She raised her chin and tried for a smile. "What exactly are we waiting *for*?"

He dropped the files next to him on the little couch and stood up. "Don't get me wrong, Val, and, please, don't bother with any complexes you might be considering." His eyes gleamed with mild humor that seemed to poke at both of them.

"And here I was all set to storm off to my room in tears of self-hatred. I've been *spurned*."

He was just inches from her now and looking into her eyes. But not touching. It was clear that he had no intention of touching her, either. "I want you so bad it's driving me nuts."

"*Bu-ut?*"

"But you're playing." His gaze caressed hers, and his voice was soft. He wasn't accusing, just stating facts.

"Playing is wrong?"

"Not at all. I'm just having a hard time telling the difference between Val as Miss Scarlet and Val the woman. At least as far as you and I are concerned."

"You think I'm faking something?"

"Playing games at the very least."

"How lovely."

"Now, I'm not objecting so much to the games as maybe the reason for them." He shrugged, only half-apologetic. "What can I say? I'm the cautious type. I have to wonder why you need the facade and what's really behind it."

She tipped her chin even higher. "Oh, baby, that cautious stuff will sweep a girl off her feet every time."

"See? That's the kind of thing I mean." He studied her eyes, not smiling and not frowning. "Instead of getting a real response from you, I generally get teasing."

"'No teasing, no playing, no flirting, but, yeah, I want you real bad, Val.' And *who* did you say was playing games?" She gave him a pointed look, her voice cool. "And, since we're being all open and honest, I bet this about-face has something to do with your ex-girlfriend. I suppose I'm paying for her stupidity?"

"I don't mean to play games with you. I'm trying to be honest, and if you think that's easy, guess again." Jack looked uncomfortable for a moment. "Yeah, maybe I am cautious because of her, too, but then I haven't had much of a social life since Chicago. I'm a little rusty. It probably shows."

"Okay. So let's keep it simple, then. What exactly do you want from me, Jack?" She tried to keep her voice level, but even she could hear the nerves twanging around the edges.

"Just you, Val. Can you just be you? Cut out the vampy act—you don't need it—and simply be *you* when we're alone together?" He gave her a wistful look. His unexpected sincerity cooled Val's impatience. And even made her ache a little.

His lips twisted in a half grin. "I think I've only seen the real you a few times now. When you clubbed me with the baseball bat and were so rattled you forgot to cover your butt. Then there was the bravado and the Come as You Died party idea. That was a blending of you and your vampy alter ego." His eyes were shrewd. "I liked it."

Her heart stuttered. *Facade? What facade?* If that's what she wore, it was pretty damn transparent. Jack seemed to see right through her. Unnerving. "You sound like you've been studying me. Analyzing me."

"Oh, I have been. More than I like. You drive me crazy on a regular basis. I'm just trying to figure out why."

At least they were back on more familiar ground. She tried out a smile. "Lucky for you, I believe I've just offered to do something about that."

"Yeah." He looked almost pained. "Really, *really* wish I could take you up on that, too."

"So why don't you?" She tried to hold the seductive voice, but it came out with a bit of an edge to it—maybe because he was really pissing her off with the rejection that was already echoing in her ears.

"When I make love with you, Val, there won't be any secrets between us, and we'll both know where we stand. You won't regret that, I promise you. Meanwhile…" He shook his head. "It's going to be me and the shower."

Yeah, him and the shower. So all she could hope for in the way of fantasy fodder was sexy Jack Harrison with pruny fingers. Gee, a new low.

"VAL, DIDN'T YOU USED TO DATE Ray Guzmano? On *Worlds of Passion*?" Lillian frowned at Val over the lenses of her glasses.

She was reading the morning paper while Val pretended to prioritize her to-do list. In reality, Val could hardly keep her mind off the man sitting next to her. Jack was acting as though that incident in her office yesterday had never happened. As though the scene afterward had never happened.

"I dated Ray, but it's been years. Why?"

Lillian slid the paper across the table to Val, and Jack stood up to peer over her shoulder while she read.

"An accident on the set. Right here in St. Louis." Val glanced up. "That's *right*. They've been filming here all week. I'd forgotten." Val returned her attention to the article. "This says he fell down a few flights of stairs."

"Probably tripped over his own ego," Lillian commented scathingly.

Val choked back a giggle. "*Lillian*. He's unconscious and might be for days yet. Have you no shame?"

"Well, he let *you* go easily enough. That makes him stupid and unworthy in my book." Lillian took the newspaper back and continued reading.

Val met Jack's eyes, and though he suppressed a grin, his eyes twinkled with it.

"Shameless sadists. Both of you." Val shook her head, trying to maintain a serious face.

"I didn't say a word." Jack looked innocent.

"Not out loud, you didn't."

"Any guy who performs a total eclipse could probably use a little humbling." Jack shrugged and headed off for her office.

Val watched him go, her heart lightening. He'd taken obscene joy in hearing that the man who had outshone her had tumbled down the stairs. And she was dysfunctional enough to enjoy it. Especially after yesterday's rejection.

She wasn't blind, though. He was measuring her still. He wasn't sure if he could trust her any further than the ex-girlfriend. Comparisons were *such* fun.

"Have you seen my scissors lying around anywhere?" Lillian murmured absently. "You know. The ones with the soft leather grips on them. I always have them."

Val thought briefly. "Blue handles, right? Not lately."

"Hmm." Lillian stared off into space. "I've meant to replace them just because. Maybe I should do that now."

"Think the bride has them?"

"Maybe. Mischievous little thing."

"And increasingly mercenary. So far I'm missing a pen, a mug, a necklace, the cameo and, as of yesterday morning, a valuable edition of the collected works of Shakespeare. Bound in indigo, of course." Val frowned. "I forgot to tell Jack about the book. Remind me."

"Of course. So tell me, dear." There was a lilt in Lillian's voice that served as its own warning. Val's aunt was occasionally too perceptive and, more than occasionally, not willing to ignore the elephant taking up squatters' rights in their kitchen. "What's going on with you and our handsome detective?"

"Who, Jack?"

"Do you know of another?"

Val made a rude noise and propped her elbows on the table. "I don't even know the one we've got."

Lillian mulled that over. "Things aren't working out? But why?"

"The man has baggage, and I too closely resemble it."

"I see. So what does this particular baggage involve?"

"He has this business-and-pleasure problem. The two don't mix. Apparently, the last lady he tried to mix it up with caused him a lot of heartache—not that he's sharing any details. He's simply assuming I'm going to do the same."

"That hardly seems fair."

"No kidding. The man doesn't trust me even on a basic level. Just continues to probe and prod at my psyche, while he half scowls at me in that way he has. Then I go and drool some more. It's revolting. I have to stop."

"You want to give up on him?"

"Well, it looks like I don't have a choice in the matter. I can't exactly force the guy to like me."

"Oh, please. Jack Harrison can't keep his eyes off of you."

"That doesn't mean he's going to do anything about it."

Lillian smiled craftily. "If the man's interested enough, there won't be a blessed thing *he* can do about it."

"Really." Val's eyes narrowed. "You wouldn't by any chance be planning on nudging things along, would you?"

"Oh, not me, darling. *You.* I'm just saying that if he has feelings for you, it's only a matter of time, patience...and exposure to you. He won't be able to help himself."

Val grinned, feeling lighthearted all of a sudden. Lillian was right. If Jack had feelings for her—and damn it all, he'd admitted he had the hots for her and found her mildly entertaining—then fighting it wasn't going to work. Not in the least.

8

"How do I look, Jack?" Valerie struck a pose in the candlelight of the Longstreet Inn's stately library. The salons and sitting areas were already beginning to bustle with conversing guests, busy caterers and serving staff.

It was October 2. A good day to die?

Val expected her big grandfather clock to chime doom on the hour, every hour. Buzzards probably circled overhead. Were there buzzards in Missouri? Who knew. Who cared?

"You look ghastly." Jack gave her a solemn look, but his eyes twinkled. "Beautiful, too."

"Excellent. A girl wants to look her best on the day of her very own funeral." Her smile firmly in place, Val smoothed the material of her blue satin sheath down her sides and hips. More gently, she tugged at the bodice, making minor adjustments to the plastic dagger protruding from her bloodstained chest.

"So I supposedly did that?" Jack raised an eyebrow at the gore-encrusted weapon.

"Yep. Right before you swallowed lead. Tragic, isn't it?"

Jack lightly touched his fingers to the rubber prosthesis affixed to the back of his head. Thanks to Val's makeup expert, he looked as if he'd literally blown his brains out. "You are *such* a fun date."

She grinned. "Hey, I am, aren't I? This would be our first real date. How romantic."

Jack just shook his head and trained his attention on a group of guests who'd just arrived. "What the hell—"

Valerie saw her landscaper and started giggling. "I love it." A handheld plastic garden rake dangled from temple to shoulder, its sharp tines seemingly embedded in William's scalp. When she waved to catch his attention, he grinned.

Jack grunted. "It's shameless."

"Of course it is. This whole party is. That's the *point*."

"I wasn't talking about his costume, at least not that way. That kid is infatuated with you. He's trying to impress you."

"Or maybe he's taking this twisted opportunity to advertise his services?" She indicated the landscaping logo on the T-shirt William wore. Granted, it dripped with fake blood, but the lettering was still legible.

Jack nodded a grudging concession.

"Valerie." A disapproving voice came from behind them. "Appalling party you have here. But I suppose I must commend you for originality."

Valerie pivoted and smiled. "Mrs. Burlington. So is that an official review? At last?"

"Hardly."

"Well, I'm still glad you made it to the party. Maybe you'll visit us in an official capacity sometime soon."

Phyllis Burlington just grunted noncommittally.

Val felt her smile slipping and searched desperately for something else to say. Mrs. Burlington's makeup was heavier than usual, her complexion rendered even pastier by heavy powder in a shade too pale for her coloring. She looked dead—which was the point of the party, after all. Val gestured gamely. "I love your costume. It's so subtle. Poisoning?"

Mrs. Burlington gave her a glacial look. "I'm not wearing a costume."

Valerie laughed, inwardly kicking herself. "Of course you're not. It was just a joke. I know you have a lovely sense of humor, but I guess mine wasn't quite on target this time. No offense intended."

"Of course." And if looks alone could kill, Val was as good as buried now. Just in time for the funereal festivities.

"Great. So—" Val turned to Mrs. Burlington's escort, scrounging up another pleasantry, then froze. *"Henri?"*

Her former chef appeared to be gloating. Why would that be? Could be he was relishing the well-chewed foot sticking out of her mouth still? And remembering how she'd fired him?

Henri nodded condescendingly. "I'm in costume, too. I believe I'm the chef that gave everyone food poisoning." He raised his eyebrows. "And later expired due to extreme shame?"

"Now there's one you don't hear every day." Valerie could have kissed Jack for his comment. In addition to his subtle humor and handsome looks, his timing was absolutely exquisite.

"I don't believe we've met?" Jack smiled at them, while Valerie performed simple introductions. "Mrs. Burlington, I've read your columns."

"Why, thank you." Mrs. Burlington warmed to Jack, while Val pondered his pandering motives with concern.

"Yes, it was very educational. I had no idea that reviewers actually specialized to the extent you do."

Mrs. Burlington blinked in confusion. "I'm sorry?"

Val stared pointedly at Jack. He didn't even glance at her.

"I'm talking about the sort of restaurants and hotels you review. You seem to patronize only a certain caliber. Or style." Jack looked guilelessly intrigued. Enthusiastic, even.

Val wanted to kill him.

His enthusiasm rose, as though he was putting pieces together into an exciting, logical whole. "I guess you and all the other reviewers in town get together and organize it that way. Some do variety. Some do smaller places. And you do…well, *chain* types."

Valerie cringed. The man was sticking up for her *now*, of all times. Where was all this blasted loyalty when he decided to accuse Val of *fraud*? No, he had to come down on a reviewer Val still hoped to woo into her corner. No chance of that happening now. Interfering male.

Phyllis Burlington nearly quivered in her outrage. "I cover a *broad range* of establishments. And no other reviewer in town has the same standing in this field as I do. I pride myself on the variety of my reviews."

"Oh. All right." He gave her an obviously placating smile that said he'd believe whatever he liked and simply agreed with her now to prevent further upset.

Mrs. Burlington narrowed her eyes at him. "You and Valerie seem awfully close."

"Like she said, I like to lend my expertise to her guests. Pro bono, of course. It's purely for my own entertainment."

"Oh, really." Her gaze shifted to Valerie with enough contempt to make Val feel like streetwalker material. Screw that. These two *both* needed rocking back on their heels.

Val forced a laugh. "Oh, Mrs. Burlington. Surely you're

not thinking what you *seem* to be thinking. No, that must be my own dirty mind that would suspect you of suspecting. Oh." She turned to Jack in discreet inquiry. "Should I just tell her? Or would you be too embarrassed?"

He gave her a startled look.

"You know, the *problem?* Oh, I'm sorry," she whispered. "I'm talking too loudly. Not something you want to get around, right?"

"I...maybe not?"

"It's nothing to be ashamed of. Really." She smiled encouragement at him, before turning back to Mrs. Burlington. "Not that it's logical in an *evolutionary* sense, though. I mean, why would Mother Nature give a man *two?* Especially when neither one works the way it should. I would think natural selection *alone* would..." She shrugged helplessly.

While Mrs. Burlington's eyes rounded—as did Jack's—Val just averted her gaze and fanned her hot cheeks. She murmured to Jack, "I'm sure your secret's safe with Mrs. Burlington, though. Shh."

Val tugged on Jack's arm and he followed, woodenly.

"You just had to do that. Didn't you." He spoke low.

"*Weelll.* Okay, yeah, I did. I appreciate your efforts on my behalf, but I like to handle my *own* business, thanks."

"And you couldn't just say so?"

"I did try, but then... Ah, what can I say? A little gremlin possessed me for a moment. I understand insanity runs in the family. You won't mind too much, will you?"

"Two? And *neither* works? The fact that you could even make up something like that. It's— That's—*diabolical.* Twisted. *Unnaturally* cruel."

"I know." She smiled sadly. "Even worse, I'm in no position to know if it's true or not."

He gave her a threatening look. "Hey, any time you want to play show-and-tell, I'm all yours."

"Oh, so that's what it takes? A challenge to your masculinity? How mature of you." She glanced over his shoulder, an innocent look on her face. "Oh, hello, Simone."

"Valerie. Hello, Jack."

Jack stepped warily to the side before turning around.

"Excellent costume." Valerie nodded approvingly and forced a smile. It was hard, after all, to maintain a sense of humor when Simone, dressed mostly in see-through black lace, looked as if she wanted to gobble up Val's escort.

Simone swept her hands over her weblike sleeves and gave Jack a smoldering look. "I'm the Black Widow."

"But that's a murderer." Val frowned in mild protest.

"Darling, you *know* I'm no sheep." Simone enunciated with a patronizing lilt. "Just because you're flushing out a predator doesn't mean I can't keep him or her company."

"*There's* a lovely thought. Heaven forbid my stalker should feel lonely."

As a precaution she felt any responsible boss should take, Val had reluctantly told her staff about the stalker notes and her intentions as soon as she had decided to throw this party. She supposed she should have known Simone wouldn't be able to resist prodding that delicate point in the name of dramatic irony. It was center stage for that woman, at all costs.

Simone sighed. "Don't get your panties in a wad. I'm also a beauty casualty." She pivoted to demonstrate how her side-swept hairstyle showcased a dainty pair of scissors protruding from her bared neck. "Just my way of showing support."

"Ah." Val nodded appreciatively then frowned. "Aren't those Lillian's scissors?"

"Well, I certainly wasn't going to sacrifice *mine* for the cause. She should buy some new ones, anyway. Owning anything with blue on it in this place is sheer lunacy." She rolled her eyes. "These turned up on my dressing table this evening. I have no idea how they got there."

Val sighed. "Lillian was looking for them."

Jack looked startled. "Missing scissors?"

"Dum-dum-*daaaaaaah*," the actress intoned in a spooky purr of a voice. "The ghost strikes again."

"Did your *ghost* return anything else?" Jack asked.

Val glanced at him. "Not lately."

"Interesting."

"Well, time to mingle." Simone smiled mostly at Jack and sauntered to a nearby group, where Mrs. Burlington and Henri mingled with local businessmen.

"You know, she still gives me the creeps." Jack grimaced.

Val relaxed. "Survival instincts. Don't ignore those."

"Not to worry. I think she eats men for breakfast."

"Poor Jack."

Jack shook his head and settled a hand on her waist to guide her onward. "So tell me. Does it strike you as odd that nothing else has turned up—like it usually does—except Lillian's scissors? Everything else is still missing."

Val shrugged off his concern. "I'm assuming I'll still find the other stuff. I just haven't looked in the right place yet. You heard Simone. The scissors turned up in a place Lillian wouldn't touch with a ten-foot pole."

"So. Simone's scary as hell. Mrs. Burlington and Henri seem to enjoy spewing venom. Do you have any *nice* friends?" Jack asked, setting aside the ghost.

"Of course I do. You're just visualizing all of them as

stalkers, thieves and potential murderers at the moment. I imagine that's coloring your opinion."

He gazed around the room. "Mandy looks normal enough."

"She is." Val smiled fondly at Mandy, a hardworking actress whose healthy good looks were marred by an eyeball dangling to her cheekbone. A particularly ugly way to die.

"And your other actors. Chad and Brad—brothers, right?"

Val spoke in a low, spooky purr. "Even better, they're fraternal twins. They have that whole twin ESP thing going."

"Sounds useful."

"They're also very nice guys and serious about their work. Reliable, creative, willing to kill in a variety of ways. Lillian adores working with them." Val waved at the two men, who wore a double-ended noose looped around each of their necks.

Jack frowned. "I don't get it. A double hanging?"

"Sure. You just toss one guy over a high, sturdy tree limb..." She left the rest to his grisly imagination. "I think it's supposed to be a twisted Freudian thing, too, though." She cocked her head appraisingly.

Jack studied them a moment longer, then gazed around the room at various other corpses, discreetly placed "evidence" and instruments of death. The weapons and blood were obviously fake, but the effect was gruesomely realistic. Val had some real talent working for her. "You know, this party could really get to you after a while."

"A bit much, huh?" She grinned. "That's the idea. Maybe we can eliminate my stalker through simple overkill."

Jack groaned. "Weren't punsters put to death at one time?"

"Probably." She gestured in apology and sent him a bright glance she couldn't quite sustain. "I think I have that nervy punchy thing going again. Today's date and all."

Jack gave her a concerned look. "You know, if this stuff is starting to unnerve you, we can call the party off or even just skip out on it. You don't have to put yourself through this."

"No. I appreciate it, Jack, but I just can't let him win. This is *my* party now—not his." She took his arm. "Stealing his theme was supposed to be an insult, remember? A victory over bad-mannered bullies everywhere."

"Or maybe a foolhardy challenge?"

"Spoilsport." She smiled at him. "Come on, let's go find my aunt. I know she's got to be reveling in all the deadly festivities." She glanced around the party until her gaze lit on the older woman and she tugged Jack in her wake.

"Aunt Lillian!" Valerie checked out Lillian's costume then started laughing. "Let me guess. The pen is mightier than the sword?"

"But of course, dear." Lillian wore a complacent expression to match her glamorous attire: a satin and black lace dress with a silvery fur stole draped from her elbows. Protruding from her bosom was an old-fashioned quill pen. Fake blood seeped from the "entry" point and lightly matted the otherwise graceful white plume that curled at an oddly flattering angle across her clavicle and shoulder. The effect was that of an obscene brooch. Given the pride Lillian took in her research, Val was quite certain the pen was positioned at a precisely lethal angle and location.

"Lillian, you do have style." Jack spoke with amused certainty and no little awe.

"Why, thank you, dear." She preened. "I consider it part

of my job description, though. It contributes to the inn's mystique."

"Naturally."

"Aunt Lillian, you wouldn't know how to lack mystique. You can draw eyes and curiosity without even trying."

"I don't know, Valerie. I think I'm upstaged this evening." Lillian nodded toward Simone. "That girl just can't help herself, can she? The invitation clearly stated *victims*, not perpetrators. She just has to steal the show every time."

Val studied the actress. When Simone happened to glance her way, Val smiled pleasantly but Simone seemed too distracted by conversation to respond. "Simone's just hungry for the spotlight. I can't fault her for that. Since it's the Longstreet Inn's spotlight she generally dominates."

"She does draw the men in, I'll give her that." Lillian glanced knowingly at Val. "I wouldn't be surprised if this event of yours invites a lot of future business. We should keep the reservation book handy."

Val waved a hand with breezy confidence. "Not to worry. I have it set up in my office, all ready to go."

"There's a surprise." Jack grinned ruefully.

"Now, come into the light and let me look at you, Valerie." Discreetly sliding her glasses onto her nose, Lillian stepped back a pace to survey her niece. Slowly, wistfully, she smiled. "Oh, Val, darling, you look just like your mother tonight."

"Um, I have this bloody dagger in my chest?" Val gestured toward the gory distraction between her breasts.

"No, I mean *you*. The costume doesn't count. You're just glowing and golden and so poised. I believe, if you wanted, you could draw the spotlight all to yourself. Just like she always could. It was as though she had this switch she could throw whenever she wished. They said that about Marilyn Monroe. When she wanted to be the star, she just radiated *star*...and there it was. That quality dazzled your father every time. Dazzled everyone, really."

Staring at her aunt, Val hung on to every word. "I wish I could have seen her through the eyes of a woman. She must have been amazing."

"Oh, she was." Absently removing her spectacles and slipping them into her clutch bag, Lillian gazed at Val, obviously faraway in her thoughts, before she shook off her mood. "Why don't you two run along? Mingle or take a walk in the moonlight or something."

Val turned reluctantly to scan the room. "I guess we should mingle. It's why we threw this party in the first place."

"Sure, it is." That was Jack's mocking comment.

"Well, maybe a little thumbing of the nose at my stalker friend, too. So. Shall we?" She extended her hand in invitation.

"Lead on."

"Have fun, you two." Lillian waved them off as though sending them on a date.

A ludicrous thought, really, considering their grisly getups. Val sighed. Normalcy sounded pretty darn good sometimes. Not for too long a stretch, of course. But certainly long enough that she could concentrate on her P.I. for a while. And decide whether she could emotionally afford the man for anything beyond a lover.

"Skits?" Jack stopped and stared at the door leading to the patio. An attractive poster invited guests to participate in murder-mystery skits starting every half hour. "Why didn't I hear about this?"

"Hmm? Oh, this was Lillian's baby. She insisted. I thought it was great promotion for the mystery shows. Why? Want to participate?"

"I don't know. Do I?" He gave her a skeptical look.

She laughed. "Well, you *are* dressed for the part."

"Part? Wait a minute, Val—"

She ignored him and, glancing at the clock, realized the next skit was getting ready to start. "Come on. I dare you."

Still grumbling, he followed her. Despite his reluctance, Jack took stage direction very well, Val noted a short time later. The man could act when he let his guard down. If he had the gall to produce convincing tears on command, she'd have to kill him. Prima donna rights prevailed. *She* was the one who'd trained for this, not him.

Still, his sense of drama was a little off, Val noted with a chuckle she tried to suppress. He heard it, though, and opened one corpselike eye to glare at her. At that point, she lost it—even dropping the miniature gun disguised as lipstick she'd used to "shoot" him, and thereby spoiling the mystery.

"So much for good publicity, eh?" she murmured to him after they vacated the stage for the next batch of revelers.

"Oh, I don't know," he said with a grin. "I think you won everyone over because of it. It was fun to see you lose it like that." He chuckled. "Although maybe the multiple shootings *after* the victim was already dead—"

"—and *laughing* at me!"

"—was overkill."

"So to speak."

"Oh, good Lord." He groaned.

Giggling now, she led him toward a group of businessmen she knew vaguely. He'd been such a good sport, he deserved a little profitable networking. As they circulated the room, Val realized that Jack was getting along very well. Smiling when one man in particular seemed interested in Jack's services, Val excused herself to give them privacy.

Besides, she thought, now she could sneak off to check out the reservation book. She wandered off to her office and flipped through the sign-up sheet. Four new bookings. *Excellent.* All those brochures she'd printed up and placed in tasteful but obvious locations around the lower rooms were doing their job. She should put another stack by the door, she imagined, and set up the computer to print off another dozen or so. As the printer chugged away, she jotted down notes, follow-up calls to make. After that, she should check on—

The door slammed open and Jack barged in.

"Jack?"

He had red lipstick on his neck and panic in his eyes.

"That *woman*. She's a menace." Jack looked hot and angry and embarrassed. A truly flustered detective.

Val bit back a grin. "I thought I left you in reasonably safe hands. Drumming up business."

"Yeah, well, I was kidnapped, thanks."

"Let me guess." Val tapped a fingernail on her chin, eyeing the lipstick print. "Simone?"

"The Black Widow seeks to live up to her name. Seduce and then drain the blood from her victims."

"Detective, it looks like she was working mostly the seduction half of that modus operandi." She pointed to his neck.

Grumbling, he rubbed at his throat, smearing the lipstick further, until she handed him a tissue.

"I don't think the bloodletting was too far behind. Have you seen those claws of hers?"

Val raised an eyebrow. "I bet she'd be a real wildcat in bed. Is that what you're saying?"

He gave her a harassed look. "I don't know what I'm saying. I'm not even sure what I said to *her*. Mostly, I just ran."

Val tried not to laugh. She really did.

"Sure, *you* think it's funny. That woman does *not* take no for an answer." He scowled. "Damn it, she asked if I really had two, and would I like to give each another shot at paradise."

Val snorted and laughed until tears streamed down her cheeks. "I'm sorry, Jack. God, I thought Mrs. Burlington would have the sense to realize I was just insulting her intelligence. And if *she* didn't, you'd think Simone at least would figure it out. Then again, I'm sure Simone's a hell of a lot more worldly than I am. Do you suppose there really *are* some men out there who—"

"Val!" Jack was sputtering, caught between hilarity and outrage. "Whatever the hell she knows or believes, *I* thought she was going to rape me in the library. Thank God you don't have a dance floor set up. I don't know what would have happened if I'd been cornered into voluntarily touching her."

"I'm sure Simone would have exploded with lust, kissing and clawing, in a wild feeding frenzy." Val shook her head pityingly. "I would have had to rescue you."

"You'd rescue me?"

"Maybe."

"Really?" He looked mildly appeased.

"Or not." She grinned evilly.

"You're a cruel woman."

"Yeah." Frowning at a smear of red that was too close to his white collar, she took the tissue from his hand. Deftly, she swabbed up the residue and tossed the tissue in the trash can.

He watched her, unspeaking, the entire time. "So what would it take to get *you* to attack me like that?"

"I tried, remember? It was humbling."

"I was a blind idiot, Val. I want another shot at it."

"Why?" She felt suspicious and painfully vulnerable.

"Honestly? I wasn't up for a one-sided relationship, where you saw me as light entertainment and I was in over my head." He studied her with hushed curiosity. "But I've been watching you. And I think I've figured it out. I already knew you resort to Val the vamp whenever you're nervous or feeling exposed." He approached her carefully. "But now I get the rest of it. I make you nervous. You feel exposed around me. You feel something and you don't want me to see it."

It wasn't a question so she didn't dare answer.

"So now that I suspect we'd both be going under..."

Great. Herr Freud had been analyzing her, while she'd been checking out his butt. A girl could feel downright naked. "Thanks, but, no thanks." She smiled without humor. "I don't feel like drowning." She turned toward the door.

He caught her hand and gently drew her back. "Who says you have to drown? This doesn't have to hurt anyone."

"Honestly, Jack. All these death metaphors. It's getting grisly in here." She tried for a light tone.

"You're hiding again." He held her gaze.

She narrowed her eyes. "You know, Jack, there's such a thing as proper time and place. This is a party. I'm the hostess. I need to get back to my guests."

"Proper time and place, huh? So what was that right here in your office the other day, then? Typical office behavior?"

"That was a whim."

"So let's have some more whimsy. I'm game."

She groaned. "Ja-ack."

"I'll wear you down." It was a teasing singsong, in a softly rasping voice that tingled along her nerve endings.

She gave him a disgruntled look. "Hey. That was *my* gig."

"Now it's mine."

"Oh, so you think you'll succeed where I failed?"

He shrugged. "Bit by bit...I'll grow on you. You won't be able to resist me."

"Yeah, yeah. And then you'll be all over me like fake blood on a plastic dagger." She taunted him with fluttering lashes and a tight smile.

"Nice imagery."

"Just perpetuating the party theme."

"Come on, Val. Give a guy a break. Go out with me."

"No."

"So stay in with me."

"*No.*" She gave an exasperated laugh. "Now *move* so I can get back to my guests. I have a party to hostess, remember?"

"How could I forget? You make such a lovely corpse."

She ducked under his arm to open the door.

The rest of the evening was mostly a blur, but for the clarity of Val's memories and imaginings. The other day in her office had started out as a whim, true, but the feelings had grown into much more. They *haunted* her, and as a rule, light whimsy just lacked that haunting quality. Oh, but Jack could haunt her for a long time. And now that he'd stopped resisting her, he was damn near irresistible himself.

It made her feel too vulnerable. She wasn't sure she was brave enough for that. It was like living naked. That's what he wanted, right? Emotional nudity? Scary stuff.

She sighed, glancing at the refreshment table to check on the supply of napkins, utensils—

"Miz Longstreet, we could maybe use another bottle of chianti. More vodka, too, just in case." A bartender, hired for the evening, gave her an inquiring smile.

"Are you completely out?"

"No. Might not even need them. But just in case."

She nodded. "Better too much than too little."

"Want me to get those? They're downstairs, right?"

"Hmm?" She glanced around and saw a group of laughing women with empty martini glasses headed toward them, probably looking for refills. "No, that's okay. I'll take care of it. Thanks."

She turned and hustled toward the double doors, smiling and making quick pleasantries along the way, then slipped down a hallway toward the back of the house and the wine cellar.

Just as she was opening the basement door, it occurred to her that she was crazy. This was, after all, October 2. No matter how much she doubted the so-called stalker's intentions, her current position and setting were just too slasher movie to ignore. Gloomy basement, deserted and dimly lit hallway. Noise everywhere but here.

Nope. No how, no way was she going into that basement. Not alone. Fictional freaks like Freddy and Jason existed for a reason—mostly to teach people how *not* to act like idiot teenage victims of serial killers.

With visions of hockey masks and blade-fingered gloves dancing in her head, she moved to close the door again when she felt a hard shove from behind and stumbled dangerously close to the basement stairs. "*Hey—*" She glanced around blindly, trying desperately to regain her balance before—

Another shove, harder, and she pitched helplessly forward. As the stone and cement flooring seemed to rise up to meet her, she windmilled her arms, seeking and finding a handhold on the railing. But it collapsed. She had time only to cover her head and close her eyes before she bumped, rolled and careened down the stairs into painful darkness.

9

"UGH." VAL GRUNTED when she finally hit bottom and stopped. Dizzy. Her entire body was numb or starting to ache already. To move or not to move. She voted not. Moving could only be painful.

"Valerie? *Val*—" A man's voice, shouting.

She winced. "Jack." The word emerged as a croak, rather than the reassurance that might halt further shouting.

What followed was a string of curse words so loud and long it nearly drowned out the stomping of big feet down the stairs.

"Oooh...*please*... Shut *up* already." She groaned.

"You're conscious. Are you okay? What hurts?" He knelt beside her. He was so vital, energetic, too *damn* healthy. And *loud*.

"My head, mostly. Please...could you cuss a little softer? I think I'm broken. Lots of bruises."

"Sure. Anything." His voice sounded hoarse. "Just don't move."

"No worries. Not moving. Afraid to move."

"I'm just going to check you out."

"God. You're going to make a move on me *now*?" She half laughed in an attempt to settle her nerves. "Your timing sucks."

"Yeah. Thought I could catch you at a weak moment." He chuckled, but it was a hollow sound, as he gently ran his hands along limbs and torso. "Lots of bruises I'm sure, but nothing seems broken..." Then he probed her scalp.

"*Ow.*"

"A knot already starting here. But no blood. Look at me."

She did so, dazedly.

"Wait a minute. You got a flashlight anywhere? Don't move. I'll call the paramedics and—"

The door slammed and the basement went pitch-black.

"What the hell?"

"Wow. I must have really pissed somebody off," she muttered as Jack gently disentangled himself from her.

"Don't move. I'll be right back." She heard scraping and the rustle of clothing then distinct steps up wooden stairs.

"Don't you dare leave me alone down here." She tried to sound threatening, but her voice quavered.

"Damn it, Val. I wish you'd worried about that a few minutes ago. Good thing I saw you talking to that bartender."

"Yes. Dumb move. I'd already figured that out and was communing with the ghosts of Freddy and Jason before you got here. I get it." Her voice sounded weak to her own ears.

"What?"

"Never mind. It won't help my cause."

"We need light and help. Let me—" His voice was coming from the top of the stairs now, and she heard the door rattling on its hinges, then a fist pounding against it. "Damn it." Jack raised his voice. "Hey. *Open the damn door.* Hello!"

A few more minutes of that, and Valerie raised her own voice. "Light switch. On your right."

A rasping, a slap, then a click. A dim glow lit the stairs.

"And, before you start pounding again...I hope you realize no one will hear you," Valerie said. "That door's older than Satan himself. Heavy oak. Probably petrified into stone by now. And with all the noise from the party going on upstairs. Just let me—" She reluctantly, carefully slid her hands down and tried to pry herself off the floor. "Oh, God. This is going to hurt like hell in the morning."

She gingerly curled upward, the stupid dagger prodding her chin. Given her fall down the steps, it was a darn good thing she'd opted for safety over authenticity. Plastic was good. She couldn't even fathom rolling down the stairs with a real dagger—even one chopped off at the tip and dulled along the edge—dangling from her chest. Sliced and diced and—

"Ah, Val. *Don't move.* I told you—"

"I need to move if we're ever going to get out of here." She tested one leg and then the other. "I seem to be attached still—" she groaned "—to most everything I had before that *idiot* shoved me down the stairs."

"Shoved? You were *shoved?*" Jack stared down at her.

She recalled the distinct impression of warmth and pressure on her back. Hard, intentional and twice. "Definitely shoved."

"And now the door's locked."

"I have an enemy."

"Yeah. Your stalker. Apparently he means business."

"Maybe. Or maybe... *No.*" It was too weird, but—

"What?"

"It's just that I'm not the first woman to fall down these steps. The last one was supposed to get married."

"No wedding?"

"Nope. She fell to her death. Um. Right about *here*." She felt chilled suddenly. "I'm going to move now."

"Val—"

"No. Really. She fell *right* here. See that stain? They never could get the blood out. I'm wearing blue. Damn it, I'm wearing *blue*. Hello." Near panic, she raised her head and gazed around the dim basement. "Yo, brain-dead bride. It's not going to work, okay? I can pretty much guarantee that taking me down with you—even if I'm wearing blue—just cannot bring you good mojo. Or whatever the hell it is you ghosts look for after your death. Your groom's long dead, anyway. There's no point in searching for blue anymore and—"

"*Val*. Take it easy. You sound a little off."

No doubt. She blinked. "So maybe I'm a little shaky."

She leaned against the wall and Jack made his way downstairs to join her. Eyeing her with concern, he cupped her shoulders. "Just don't make any sudden movements for a while. Why don't you tell me more about this ghost you think shoved you down the stairs?"

"Gee. Why do I get the feeling you're just humoring me?"

"Got me. I wanted to hear a good ghost story." Peering around the gloom, he focused on an old couch against the back wall and carefully led her toward it. She waited while he whisked off the sheet that had covered it, then lowered herself gratefully onto the faded cushions. Sure beat sprawling all over the cement floor.

"So." Jack prompted her as he sat down. "The ghost?"

"Right. Eleanor Baxton."

"A relative of yours?"

Val nodded. "Distantly, by marriage. Grandma was into all that genealogy stuff, so I'm sure she could have explained it much better. She loved her ghosts." Val looked sad for a moment. "So. Eleanor. She was the youngest in a family of six and died as a young woman almost a hundred years ago. She was born in the master bedroom upstairs, grew up in this house and was all set to even get married here. But she had a fatal flaw."

"Don't they all? And what was Eleanor's fatal flaw?"

"Indecisiveness. As I understand it, she searched the house up and down for the perfect something borrowed, something blue, something old, something new."

"Ah."

"Yeah, she only got as far as blue. She was headed down here, several blue items in hand, to go through old trunks looking for the perfect blue something. But these stairs…" She glanced up at them, warily. "Well, as I understand it, the original ones were even more treacherous than this set, and I'm sure she was hurrying and distracted—"

"And so she fell to her death."

"That's the story. The rest of it is that she continues to wander around this place, looking for something blue. So we have blue things that seem to go missing for a while and then turn up in strange places a few days later. Like she's picking up and discarding. Indecisive, even after death."

"Sounds hellish. So you thought maybe she'd graduated from searching out blue accessories to knocking off a woman dressed all in blue? Now there's frustration for you."

"So maybe I freaked a little. What do you expect? Lying in her long-ago body prints at the bottom of the steps, wearing the blue she obsesses over… It was bizarre."

"Of course." He was humoring her again. "And you had every right to confront her with the situation."

She scowled.

"So is Eleanor your only ghost?"

"No. Just the most beloved. We also have a guy—Eleanor's youngest brother—who killed himself in one of the bedrooms upstairs a couple years after she died. Right around two in the morning, people sometimes hear groaning and footsteps in that part of the building. Come to think of it, though, I heard weird tapping this morning. Like someone tapping his toe. Not impatient, just fidgeting. Happy fidgets." Val shook her head. "It was probably just Lillian up writing. Anyway, legend has it that he's pacing to try to relieve himself of the voices and depression that eventually drove him to take his life.

"Another Baxton died under strange circumstances a couple decades later. Eleanor's nephew. He died in the library—our current war room—from a heart attack apparently brought on by shock. It was obvious someone had dropped by, stayed to have cigars and drinks with him, then shared news ugly enough to send him into cardiac arrest.

"So now pens tend to go missing, books fall off shelves for no apparent reason, all that good stuff. I understand the guy loved his books. He studied them and wrote little notes in the margins." She smiled. "It's been a couple of weeks since something like that happened, though. I kind of enjoy that one. I never know what he's going to write next."

"How do you know all this?" He gave her a dubious look. "Couldn't that last guy have just died of a simple heart attack, no mystery about it?"

"There have been stories passed down, diaries that have long since perished or disappeared."

"So we're talking simple hearsay?" He looked skeptical.

She rolled her eyes. "Is there no romance in your soul?"

"Not a bit. Instead, I have a very good brain in my head."

"Smart-ass."

"Yep." He studied her face. "Your color looks better."

She nodded. "I'm going to be sore, but I think I'm okay."

"Good. Just take it easy."

She slid off the couch carefully. "Why don't we see about getting ourselves out of here?"

"Sounds good. You supervise and I'll do the legwork."

"Okay." Even suspecting it would be fruitless, Val directed Jack to the top of the stairs, where he felt around in the crevice she described for the spare key she kept behind the banister. The crevice was empty.

No big surprise. Val sighed. "There's also an exit to outside from here, but it's completely impassable without a key. A smart detective I know insisted on a new steel door and dead bolt. But I don't have a key or card on me."

"Yeah, that detective's a regular brainiac, isn't he." Jack looked harassed.

"We can try the window maybe."

"There's a window? Why didn't you say so?"

She made a face. "You won't like this one. The Dumpster is in front of it. Blocking it, in fact. Unless—"

He checked out the tiny window, discovered the Dumpster was still pushed up against it and too heavy to move. The new door proved impossible to force, too, Jack grimly concluded. Good, high-quality doors. A guy just couldn't win for trying.

"So we wait?" Val asked in a level voice.

He shrugged. "We could try pounding on the door to upstairs in the hope that someone happens back here, but—"

"Not likely." She sighed. "I don't suppose you have a phone on you?"

Jack was already shaking his head. "Gun's upstairs, too, for all the good it would do me against the doors from hell."

"I don't care. I still say a real gun has no place at a party." Val muttered her side of an argument they'd had earlier that day. Then she frowned at a sudden thought. "Hey, there is the bartender, though. He knew I was headed down here."

"We should be missed after a while then, right?"

"Except he was almost at the end of his shift, so he may have left by now. Young guy and temporary, too. Not sure how reliable he is."

She paused, considering their options. "Lillian will miss me. Maybe not tonight, though. I think she has some misguided notion about where I might be sleeping." She gave him an annoyed look he probably didn't deserve. "So she'll discreetly *not* seek me out tonight. But I know she'll miss me come morning and start looking."

"So we should expect to spend the night down here."

"Yes." She closed her eyes. "And this is the time when all women suddenly feel the urge to use the facilities. Mostly because there are no facilities to use."

Not the reaction he was expecting, but certainly preferable to hysteria. He felt that familiar, disorienting flash of amusement. "Like taking a long car trip across the open plains?"

"While it's pouring, of course, just to rub it in. Or maybe a long hike through the woods while in mixed company." Her eyes blinked open, reflecting an amusement similar to his own.

"I see."

"Females require a little more maintenance. Guess I'll—we'll—have to make do with what we can find. There should be plenty of food and bottled water down here, at least." She turned quickly. "Let me just check—" Then she swayed and stumbled. He caught her.

"Damn it. Keep this up and you're going to pass out on me." He scowled at her, his eyes dark with concern. "You should be letting me do all the legwork. Why aren't you sitting?"

"Because I thought it might be fun to see if we had enough food and water for the night? I just stumbled, for Pete's sake. Get a grip." She pulled free and tried to walk away but couldn't deny lingering light-headedness.

"Val." Jack grabbed her arm. "Take it easy. Please. You've been moving around like nothing happened, when you could very well have hairline fractures, a concussion, internal injuries—"

"Honestly, I'm fine, Jack." She tried a reassuring smile, but it was strained with impatience. "When did you turn into a worried old woman?"

"Since you scared the hell out of me. Val, I swear to God. When I saw you lying there at the bottom of the steps. Not even moving." He shook his head and looked away a moment. "Hell, I thought I was too late."

"Oh, Jack." The look in his eyes was enough to stop her breath. That was a lot of intensity for subtle, laid-back Jack Harrison. The man felt emotion—and deeply. He was simply good at disguising it.

Overwhelmed, she stopped fighting him and let him guide her back to the couch. She had the feeling he needed to help her more than she needed to be helped. "Honestly, Jack, I'm okay. I swear. Bruised and sore, but okay. I managed to grab onto the rail, and it slowed my fall. So it wasn't as bad as it looked. I was mostly shaken up."

"Yeah, I saw the busted rail." He lowered himself onto the couch next to her and rubbed at his face, obviously trying to regain his cool. "I know. Rationally, I know. I checked for broken bones. You don't have signs of a concussion. I just—"

"Yeah. It spooked me a little, too."

"You were shoved down the stairs and it just 'spooked you a little'?" He gave her a wry look. "God, I don't know about you, but I could really use a drink right now."

She stared at him, incredulous, and then she was laughing. It was probably due to the strain of minor things like someone pushing her with the intent to injure or kill, but she laughed like a rattlebrained idiot until Jack was bending close, his eyes wide with concern.

"Val, you're scaring me again."

"Just savoring the irony. You see, you've just hit on the one thing I can easily get my hands on right now." Cupping his cheeks, she tugged him close for a smacking kiss. "Know what's just around that corner?"

"An unlocked door?"

She grinned, a gleeful conspirator, and whispered. "The wine cellar."

"Well, why didn't you say so?"

"It's right over—"

"No. Sit. Stay. I'm sure I can find it."

She rolled her eyes, but didn't move. Now that she knew how badly her fall had shaken him, it was easier to humor all the orders. Enjoy them even, in a twisted, pathetic way. "There's a pinot grigio on the left, top row, that's particularly good."

"Check." He came back, dusting off a wine bottle and raised an eyebrow. "Any idea where I can find a corkscrew, or should I play Boy Scout?"

"There might be one on top of the rack."

He rounded the corner again, she heard some shuffling, and then he returned, grinning. "Bingo. The evening's looking up." He nodded behind him. "There's a stack of old linens in one of those boxes, too. I peeked.

"And—" he cleared his throat "—as far as facilities...there's a drain back in the corner. It might do in a pinch."

She stared at him. "You've got to be kidding. A drain? I'm used to a full-blown bathroom, thanks, complete with shower, toilet and well-stocked vanity. Toilet paper, too. It's *important*, you know."

He grinned, but not without sympathy.

She sighed. "Never mind. Change the subject."

"Can I pick the subject?"

"Not until after I've had some of that wine."

Just as he extended his hand to offer her the freshly opened bottle, he frowned and pulled it back.

"What?" She scowled at him. "If anyone around here needs a drink, I'd think it would be me. I did just take a header, remember?"

"Exactly. I wonder if we should be careful, in case of a concussion or something."

"Again, I appreciate the concern, Jack, but I'm okay. Somehow, I think we would have gotten a clue by now if anything were seriously wrong with me."

"Maybe."

She smiled with soft calculation. "Let's put this a different way, then. Hand over the bottle and no one gets hurt."

He raised an eyebrow, his eyes gleaming with surprise and humor. "Hmm. Since you put it that way." Still, he was slow about handing off the bottle, his gaze firmly fixed on hers.

Sizing up her pupils, no doubt. "Quit fretting or I'll have to start doubting your masculinity." She met his eyes for a long moment. "Since we're stuck together down here for the night, I'd hate to doubt something like that."

"Really." He sat next to her. "That sounds leading to me."

"You think?" She took a swig of wine, paused to let it swirl around her tongue, then swallowed and smiled at him.

"I do think." His gaze never wavering, he took the bottle from her and carefully raised it to his own lips.

"Plan on doing anything about it?" She made it a blatant challenge, her toes curling in anticipation.

He lowered the bottle and considered her for a moment. There was definitely some heat in those hazel eyes. "I am, actually. I'm going to ask why." He set the bottle on the floor.

Disarmed, she regarded him warily. "Why what?"

"Why now, why here? Are you just killing time, Val? You know I'm not up for that."

"More games. I get it. Suit yourself, handsome."

"Ah, Val." He looked disappointed. "You're hiding."

"I thought you'd be pleased."

"Pleased that you're hiding away again?"

"I'm right here, haven't moved a muscle. I thought you'd be pleased that I'd changed my mind. My office tonight, remember?"

"Oh, I remember all right. You were breathless and big eyed and turned on. It was real."

Emotional nudity again. Oh, goody. Forcing an amused smile, she gave him a teasing, seductive look, and lowered her voice to a whisper. "'Big eyed and breathless,' huh? *Vulnerable.* Is that how you like it, Jack? You need to have me always at a disadvantage so you can be in control? Sorry. Not my style."

He gave her a searching look. "Is that how the ex-boyfriend liked it? The one who eclipsed you?"

Her gaze flickered. "I figure it was his way of gaining control of *something*, since Mommy Dearest controlled every other aspect of his life. He had to be a big old prima donna on the set, too."

"I don't want to control you, Val. I don't want to outshine you, eclipse you or stifle you in any way." He smiled at her. "You fascinate me too damn much to do without all the quirks that drive me nuts."

She was genuinely touched. "Really?" A man fascinated by her and by her quirks. An amazing concept.

"Yes, *really*. All by yourself. The twisted, gutsy you that would dream up something as ghoulish as a Come as You Died party. Then have the courage and style to actually pull it off. You're amazing. Crazy, but amazing."

Ignoring the sudden fluttering in her belly, she grinned sunnily at him. "Oh. I get it. You like dysfunctional. Turns you on, doesn't it."

He started laughing. "In you, it damn well might."

"Jack, darling, it's obvious you need help. I've been meaning to talk to you about—*mmph*." He took her mouth in a kiss so encompassing she felt mute, boneless, while blood seemed to kick up and froth in her veins. The man could kiss and then some. *Wow*.

She came up for air, sanity, *something*. "Jack—"

"Yeah. Dysfunctional." He breathed the words, hot, against her lips. "I can do dysfunctional. Shut up and kiss me, though."

"Oh. Uh-huh." She loved the way he could rile up every

nerve ending in her body. *Drowning*. Oh, yeah, she could definitely drown in this man's kisses. She loved his not-quite smiles and the rare laughter just because it was rare and therefore more precious. And such a big, noble heart. She loved—

Val pulled back, dazed by near knowledge. She couldn't, *wouldn't* accept—

"Val?"

Somehow he'd managed to lay her out flat on her back across the faded couch cushions. The plastic dagger, he'd obviously shoved to the side—along with the flaps of her dress bodice, which was currently undone. As was her front-closure bra? She laughed up at him in mild shock. "You work *fast*."

"Stealthy hands." He lowered his gaze to her bared breasts before meeting her eyes again. "Is that a problem?"

Nimble fingers. Hot mouth. Hotter body. Big, lovely heart. "No problem at all." His lips moved closer, then she simply fell into his kiss. She felt his lips curve into a grin against hers and surrendered shakily to the inevitable. She'd always known she'd be a goner if she ever got the man to smile at her.

Wallowing in the warmth that made her limbs rubbery, she slid her fingers through his hair to— "Mmmph. Jack!"

He raised heat-fogged eyes to meet hers. "Hmm? I thought—"

"Your hair."

"My hair?"

"Your brains are all over your hair." Snickering, she tugged at the rubbery mass attached to the back of his head. "It's, um..."

He looked adorably harassed. "Making you giggle?"

"Well, sort of."

He sat up and turned around. "Fine. Help me out."

"I'm not sure I can. It all depends. Oh, you're in luck." She unpinned the discreetly adhered mess and showed him the gory fake hairpiece.

He plucked it out of her hand and tossed it, even as she slid her arms around him and pulled him back down on top of her, his back to her front, spoon-style. She loved how his hair curled just the tiniest bit along his nape. It was easy to miss—but she hadn't. And now she desperately needed to kiss him there.

He shifted. "Uh, Val, this isn't going to work like—"

"Oh, *man*." She winced. "You're telling me." Val couldn't hold back a groan as his weight pressed fully into her bruised and battered body. "My leg."

"What? *Val*." Jack leaped to his feet. "Damn it. What the hell was I *thinking*? You just fell down an entire flight of stairs and now I'm—" He broke off his words to examine her leg.

"You were doing *exactly* what I wanted you to do." Val tried to smile as he gently manipulated her knee and ankle. "But I do feel like someone beat the hell out of me. Maybe…"

"No maybe about it. We'll wait." He scanned her leg. "I don't feel anything obviously broken, but no telling if you have hairline fractures or internal injuries. I'm not touching you again until after you see a doctor." He scowled. "I *mean* it."

She scowled back, mocking him. "I didn't realize you were so vulnerable to a little temptation."

"Yes, you did." He sounded annoyed.

"Poor baby." She ran a caressing gaze over his mussed

hair, those hot hazel eyes. His uncomfortable, frustrated posture.

"Val." He ground out her name a little desperately, recalling her attention from dangerous territory. "Let's just—talk. About something else. He eyed her distrustfully. "And I'll pick the subject."

"So pick." She smiled at the lust still heating his gaze.

"We have time. Lots of it. So we might as well make productive use of it." Jack turned his detective's frown on her. "Let's figure out who might have pushed you."

"Oh, Jack." So much for romance.

"No arguments. You were attacked, Val. This is more than a minor annoyance now."

"Fine. But I can tell you right now I didn't see, hear or even sense this person. It was like being shoved in the dark."

"Then we'll have to come at it from another direction. Take people and see who had opportunity and motive to do it. Let's start with the obvious. Simone. Do you think she holds a grudge? And, if so, how far do you think she'd take it?"

"I'm not sure. She's hard to read. I did, however, give her her job back. Of course, I didn't give her *you* back, so I guess that negates any good deed of mine."

Jack looked appalled. "I was never *hers* to be given back."

"Oh, yeah? Well, to her way of thinking, she's already written her name in permanent marker across your sexy butt."

"Let's leave my butt out of this, if you don't mind."

Val grinned. "Now that would be a real shame."

"Val." He gave her a warning look.

"All work and no play," she murmured in a singsong. "Jack's dull all right. Let's move on to your aunt."

Val's teasing ceased abruptly. "Let's not. She loves me like a mother would. She'd never do something like this."

"Push you? Probably not. I'm just filling in blanks right now. Besides, it's just possible that something you tell me will clear her or implicate someone else."

Val gave him a doubting look, then shrugged. "All right. I'm almost positive now that she's seeing a man. She's dressing differently, and she gets this dreamy look sometimes. I don't see her much in the evenings anymore, either." Val nodded. "A man. I'd bet on it."

"You haven't asked her directly?"

"I think she'll volunteer the information when she's ready. And I don't want to scare her off dating by pushing it. She considers herself a matriarch and an eccentric loner. I don't want to cramp her style and mistakenly talk her out of it."

"Okay. Auntie has a boyfriend. It's worth checking out."

"So are we done now?" Val raised an eyebrow. "I have other guests and other employees, but you've been through the files. I don't know anything new about them to report to you."

"Any weird noises, strange occurrences, something someone said that stood out?"

"It depends on what you consider strange. Eleanor's thievery is getting worse, but I already told you that. Oh, she took a book the other day. Forgot to tell you."

"Val—" Jack gave her a frustrated look.

"Sorry. Other than the ghost stuff...nothing springs to mind."

"All right. Once we're out of here, I'll check alibis for guests and staff and see what turns up."

"So. Since we *still* have loads of time to kill and fair is only fair, it's my turn to pick what we talk about." She smiled evilly. "And my choice of subject is *you*."

"Me?" He looked wary now. "What about me?"

"*All* about you. But starting…"

Jack closed his eyes.

"With your love life," she finished softly. "I think we're at that point where it would be good for you to tell me how the last woman in your life screwed up. That way I don't keep chewing on my toes or bouncing on sore spots."

"All right." He paused, obviously reluctant. "Her name was Linda. We were living together. This was about two years ago."

"Linda." Val nodded. "Go on."

"She was a defense attorney and her client was this…" Jack made a disgusted noise. "Well, she was representing a man I'd arrested for assault. It was a domestic situation."

She gave him a curious look. "Domestic?"

"He liked to beat up on his wife when he got pissed. I had a feeling he was going to end up killing her."

"And you were proven right?" She spoke carefully, hurting for him already.

He shrugged. "Domestic cases are a huge gray area in law enforcement. Cops have a hard time making a case that a prosecutor can take to court. For all kinds of emotional reasons, victims are often uncooperative."

Val nodded.

"Anyway, I had him in custody. I tried to argue with Linda privately that her client was probably going to go home and do a number on his wife if she got him off on bail. I thought he needed some cooling-off time while I tried to talk his wife into pressing charges. Linda listened to me, seemed to see my side, but then she asked for bail, anyway. She got it."

Val stared. She was almost afraid to ask. "And the wife?"

"She didn't die but he did put her in a wheelchair for the rest of her life before turning the gun on himself."

"Oh, Jack. God, I'm so sorry."

"Yeah."

Then her eyes widened. "They blamed *you*? That's why—"

"Not officially. Unofficially, yeah. Mixing business and private lives... Maybe I would have done something, worked Linda harder, worked the prosecutor against her more...if we hadn't been involved. Anyway, it was suggested that I resign, so I did. I held myself responsible for a while, but then gave it up for useless. I didn't shoot her, her husband did."

"Damn right you're not responsible." Val was furious.

Jack smiled a little. "You sound as mad as my father was when he left the department right after I did."

"I am angry. Hell, Jack, I know firsthand how protective you can be. You'd devote your heart and soul to a job like that. How *dare* they blame you."

"It's in the past now. And I've discovered, as a P.I., that I like being able to pick my own fights." He paused. "Even if I'm just fighting for a little old lady's lost dog."

That distracted her. "A dog?"

"A poodle. Bad sense of direction."

She chuckled and squeezed his hand. "I'm glad you told me. Thank you."

"About the poodle? No problem. Not one of my shinier moments, but it pays the bills." He glanced at his watch, but she could see a flush in his cheeks, even in the dim light, and it touched her.

Until he looked up. "And, hey, look at that. We still

have lots of time to kill." He grinned in anticipation. "My turn."

"Your turn?"

"My darling Miss Scarlet. Tell me. Did you never crave the limelight after your run on that soap opera?" His teasing faded to genuine curiosity. "I looked your mom up on the Internet. She did sound like a rising star. It also sounds like you considered following her example."

"Maybe." Val glanced down at her hands. "A little."

"Why a little?"

She shrugged. "Maybe I liked acting. Maybe I liked the stories and feeling them come to life."

"So why did you quit?"

"I didn't quit. They killed me off the show, remember?" She grinned at him. "And the timing was great. I inherited this place and a whole new career."

"And you sound…relieved as hell?"

"Oops?" She feigned guilt, though her heart tripped along in fear of his reaction. She'd often suspected her parents would have disapproved, that even her grandmother and aunt would be disappointed if they knew how little she'd craved true stardom. In actuality, she had a shopkeeper's heart and soul. She was happy to be a solid businesswoman with some questionable acting talent.

"Oh, no. I'm not through with you yet. Keep talking."

"There's nothing to tell, Jack. I'm just where I'm supposed to be. I thought I was supposed to excel as an actress, but instead, I was intended to be the Longstreet Inn and Mystery Theater's number one diva."

"No, that's your aunt." He grinned.

"You know, you could be right about that. I might have said Simone, but I do think Lillian is a better choice. Interesting. I bet she loves that and Simone hates it." She turned an intrigued look on Jack. "No wonder they dislike each other. Lillian's never trusted Simone and Simone's always, always challenging Lillian's dialogue. That's *so* interesting. I wonder what I could do with that. Aunt Lillian as diva."

Jack chuckled a little, but he was still studying Valerie. "I think I get it now."

Val raised her eyebrows.

"This place. Longstreet Inn. It's your stage, isn't it?"

"In its own way, yes. It's also my professional vocation and my home. Any problem with that?"

"Nope. And I think you'll be a huge success."

She gave him a toothy grin. "Unless, of course, a psycho stalker or a detective with a god complex blows the whistle on me, and this place goes down the tubes. I won't let anybody take Longstreet Inn from me or ruin it. This is my baby."

Jack backed off with all kinds of respect. "No problem. A man would have to be nuts to get between that look on your face and what put it there. Your inn's safe with me."

"Ah. Intelligence. Such an *attractive* quality in a man."

He shook his head and gave her an exasperated look. "Whatever does it for you, babe. Now get some rest. Morning and freedom will come soon enough and we can get you to a doctor."

"But—"

"No doctor, no…"

"Oh. Oooooh. Public servant all the way to the soft, gooey center. Right?"

"Nope. Private detective with a very private interest and a painful erection that you're only making worse."

She laughed, half outraged, until he tugged her into his arms and reclined with her snuggled close.

"*Go to sleep.*" And, surprisingly, she did. Ghosts and all.

HOURS LATER, VAL GROANED and tried to open her eyes. Moved a leg. Yelped.

"Val?"

"I'm a little sore."

"Damn. I'm sorry." He tried to shift his weight from her.

"Not you. You're great. It's the stairs, I think. My knee's a little creaky."

"And I've been lying on it all night. Damn." He eased away and stood up, while she gingerly stretched her leg.

Then she looked down at herself and couldn't help but laugh. "Some femme I make." Her dress—ruined by costume adornment, a fall down the steps, near lovemaking and use as a nightgown—was currently wadded to indecent proportions. God only knew where her bra had ended up after Jack so deftly stripped it off of her. "Ooh, *baby*. I am *hot*."

"You look sexy as hell to me."

"Yes, but you *like* dysfunctional. I'd forgotten." She let her smile warm with affection. He looked so darn cute with his hair sleep-tousled, his eyelashes at half-mast and an honest-to-God smile curving his lips.

The man seemed to have reclaimed his laughter. She liked to think she'd had something to do with that. She reached up to finger his cheekbone, her heart plunging at a furious pace.

He captured her finger to press a kiss to it. "So what do you say to getting out of here this morning?"

"Sounds like a plan. Just let me start moving." She sat up and winced.

"Hurts pretty bad, huh?"

"Just sore. Nothing serious." She tried to smooth her dress. "I still can't find my bra."

He bent to kiss her neck. "It's blue, right? Maybe Eleanor claimed it for a kinky keepsake."

She chuckled. "Maybe so. God knows it couldn't have gone far, but I even dug my fingers under the couch cushions and it wasn't there."

"Well, with any luck, we'll get out of here soon and can change into some different clothes, anyway."

"Yes, *please*." It was a heartfelt prayer. "So in the meantime, what do you have in mind?"

"Well, I was considering destroying your door."

"Hmm. Not a bad idea if you think it can be done."

"That's still in question, but I'm willing to try."

She glanced at the basement door, the railing and then at the stack of boxes below the stairs. "Except I have a better idea. You know, that key could have fallen through the stair treads when I yanked the railing free on my way down."

Jack closed his eyes. "Don't remind me."

"Sorry. Still, it is a thought."

"Yes." He focused on the banister and arrowed his gaze straight down. "So you think we should try to hunt down that key." He frowned at the boxes beneath the stairs. "It's worth a shot. No time like the present." Jack started hefting sealed boxes aside. As he did so, he bumped against a table behind him, sending a pink wooden box screeching toward the edge.

"Wait, that's—" Val reached wildly for the box, but her bodily creaks interfered with her reach, and the box toppled onto the floor with a crack. The lid was askew. "Oh, no." Val dropped to her knees, immediately wincing in pain.

"Damn it, Val. Will you *stop* overdoing it?"

"But it's her *hope* chest. It's busted." She groaned. "Eleanor will haunt me until my death now."

"Eleanor?" Jack, who'd squatted next to her, met her eyes in surprise. "This was hers?"

Val nodded ruefully. "I loved this box and played with it as a kid. But the finish was wearing off. I just wanted to make it pretty for Eleanor, but—"

He grinned. "Little girls think everything should be pink?"

"And little girls have almost no experience with painting furniture and knickknacks, so I painted it shut. Grandma... I thought she would go ballistic. She turned absolutely purple. But then she decided Eleanor might appreciate the gesture. Naturally, I had to grow up before I could appreciate Grandma's restraint. This thing would be worth a lot of money if I hadn't painted it."

He reached out and touched it. "Seal's broken now, though."

"Yeah, it is." Carefully, she raised it, wincing at the mangled hinge. "I'll have to fix— Oh, my God. Jack, *look*."

Inside the box were the blue mug, blue fountain pen, sapphire necklace, blue cameo, blue leather-bound book...and a vinyl music record? Val frowned to read the label, then laughed in wonder. "'Blue Suede Shoes.' Elvis Presley. This is Lillian's record! I wonder if she knew it was even missing."

"The record's a bit of a stretch."

Val shrugged. "I didn't make the rules." Her grin faded. "I wonder what all this means."

"That somebody stole these things and hid them here to pawn off later?" Even Jack looked baffled. "I can understand the necklace. Even the cameo. Maybe the book, and even remotely possible, that old vinyl record. But why the pen and mug?"

"If Eleanor took it—"

"Please."

"Hear me out." She gave him an impatient look, then stared at the collection. Her eyes widened. "Oh, geez. I'm getting goose bumps now." She turned to Jack. "Do you think...is there any way someone could really resolve her own problems...after *death*?" She squeaked the last word but held his gaze.

"Honestly? No. Dead is dead is dead."

"Right. No romance in your soul." She shook her head. "Here's my theory. The pacing...has turned to tapping. Books and pens aren't moving anymore. And this hope chest. You know what? I think she took care of all three of them." Val inhaled sharply and rubbed at her arms. "*God*. Goose bumps all over the place. Okay, Eleanor's brother, the suicidal guy...he's tapping. To *music*. Depression lifted. Our library ghost, Eleanor's nephew...has his book and his pen and his mug... Although who drinks coffee after death?" She waved off the tangent. "Never mind. My point is, he's happy, too.

"And even Eleanor has her something old, something new, something borrowed, something blue covered between the cameo and the necklace. One's old, one's new, both are borrowed and both are blue." She raised her eyes to meet Jack's.

"Fell hard on that head, didn't you." Jack looked unnerved. "How about sitting down for a while?"

"I'm serious, Jack. Grandma said Eleanor was a nurturer, and—" She blinked. "Oh, never mind. Moot point for the cynically minded."

"You got it, babe." He stood and pulled her gently to her feet. "Now stay here and behave so I can concentrate on finding that key. If it's down here." He frowned at the stairs, then lowered his gaze to the boxes directly beneath the stairs.

He checked first on the exposed floor and swept all smooth surfaces with his hand. Then he focused on an open, wildly disarrayed carton—directly below the crevice in which Val usually hid the key—and groaned. "This will be fun."

"Yeah. It's Lillian's stuff. She's not exactly a neat freak." Val shrugged ruefully.

Undeterred, Jack started pulling things out of the box, including a stack of loose photos he carefully shuffled to see if anything metallic fell out of them. Glancing curiously at the top one, he raised an eyebrow.

"What? Did you find something?" She glanced over his shoulder. "Oh, pictures." She smiled. "I've never seen these before." She gasped. "That's Aunt Lillian. Wow, was she hot."

Jack flipped to another photo, this time of a couple preserved forever in romantic lip-lock. "That's your Aunt Lillian again, unless I'm mistaken."

"Yeah." Still awed, Val just whispered it.

"So who's the guy she's kissing?"

"My dad."

10

"Your father and your Aunt Lillian?" Jack frowned at the photo. "Don't even try to tell me that's a platonic kiss between siblings-in-law."

"Wouldn't even attempt it." Val studied the image closely. "Unless I'm mistaken, there's some definite tongue action going on."

"Your dad and your aunt had an affair and this isn't a problem for you?"

She shrugged dismissively. "It was years and years ago. From when they were dating, before Dad married Mom."

Jack stared. "Your dad. And his future wife's sister."

"Yeah. Big soap-opera scandal, or so it could have been. Aunt Lillian was engaged to my dad, but they broke it off and he married my mom instead."

"But it wasn't a scandal."

"I'm sure there were hurt feelings, but all three got along great as long as I could remember."

Staring with interest at his unreadable expression, she raised an eyebrow and pitched her voice mockingly low. "*Or*...maybe my aunt's been hoarding her pain and jealousy for *lo*, these many years—about thirty of them, I believe—and is getting her revenge on their daughter. Demon spawn. That would be me."

"You wouldn't even discuss the possibility."

"That my aunt could be the stalker? The person who shoved me down those stairs? *Oh*, no. Not even for a minute."

"Val—"

"No. I refuse to even consider it."

"You don't have to. *I'll* consider it." Jack gave her a patient look. "And if your aunt's innocent, then me looking into it won't change anything. She'll have nothing to hide."

"Oh, screw that, Jack. Everyone has something to hide. Evidence can be manufactured, misunderstood or slanted any which way, depending on the viewer."

"Sort of like that hope chest you found, with all your blue stuff inside. Which, coincidentally, was placed right next to your aunt's stuff." He gave her a meaningful look.

"And what's that supposed to mean?" She glared at him. "Oh, no, you don't. My aunt did *not* take that stuff."

"Makes sense if you ask me."

"She didn't take it. She couldn't have."

"Why not?"

"Besides the fact that my aunt is not a thief, I know she didn't put that stuff in the chest. It was still painted shut before it fell off the table. Eleanor must have used her woo-woo-whatever to put it all in there. How else could anything get inside a sealed box?"

"Someone must **have** pried it open. It's open now."

"*It was painted shut.*" She spoke through gritted teeth. "I saw it."

"Or else just pulled shut so closely it *looked* like it was still painted shut." He regarded her patiently. "Look, I don't want her to be guilty of anything, either, Val. I like your aunt. She's too much like you for me not to like her.

Charming, a little nuts, sharp as hell. But I can't afford to ignore what I see. Coincidences usually *aren't*."

"Well, this one *is*."

"Val—"

The basement door swung open, and bright light shone through the open stair treads. "Hello? Anyone down here? Val?"

"Aunt Lillian!" Val gasped and stumbled out into the open to peer up at her aunt. "*Yes*. Hold that door!"

"Good thing I thought to look down here, then. Mandy and I have been searching for you for half an hour now."

"Jack and I have been down here since the party."

"Since the *party*?" Lillian peered down into the dim basement, as though surveying fresh and extensive evidence. "So you've been down here all *night*?"

"Yes. A very long night." Val glanced briefly at Jack before turning back to her aunt. "Someone locked the door behind us. And the extra key's missing. The one I usually hide in that crevice at the top of the stairs? It's not there anymore."

"Do tell." Lillian looked fascinated.

"Why don't we go upstairs first?" Jack suggested mildly.

"Oh, of course, of course. I'm sorry. You just both looked so serious all of a sudden I got distracted. Oh, my. All night long in this musty basement." Lillian took Val's arm as she reached the top of the stairs.

"I hadn't realized the rail was broken. Did that happen recently?" Lillian looked concerned, eyeing Jack and Valerie up and down as they passed her through the doorway.

Ignoring the rail and the disturbing memories it threatened to evoke, Val inhaled deeply. "Oh, thank God, to be out of that basement. Remind me to air that nasty place out."

"I didn't mind it." Jack murmured under his breath.

Still unnerved by his speculations against her aunt, Val barely glanced at him and ignored his provocative words altogether. "I need a hot shower. Fresh clothes. A real bed."

"First, you're going to see a doctor. Right after we—"

"A doctor?" Lillian sounded alarmed now. "What's going on? Are you sick, Val? Did you hurt yourself down there? Is that what happened to the railing? Did you bump into it? I thought maybe I'd just failed to notice it before, but—"

"Someone pushed Valerie down the stairs." Jack studied Lillian closely. "She was pushed from behind and fell from the top of the stairs all the way to the bottom. Part of the railing came down with her when she tried to break her fall."

"*Valerie.*" Lillian grabbed her niece's hands and tugged her to a chair. "Those basement steps. You could have been *killed.*"

"I'm *fine.*" She glared at Jack. "Did you have to scare her?"

Keeping his gaze on Lillian, Jack spoke quietly. "She needed to hear."

"Well, of course I did. Oh, Val. Someone pushed you? By accident, I suppose, but *still*. I mean, how could—"

"Why do you assume it was an accident?" Jack spoke sharply. "She *is* being stalked, remember? We have notes to prove someone threatened her harm on this date."

Lillian's face paled. "Yes, you do, don't you. Someone did this on *purpose*?"

Val quietly tried to reassure her aunt. "I'm okay. *Really.* It happened last night—*hours* ago. If I had any serious injuries, I'd know it by now. But Jack's right about this being intentional. I was definitely pushed. I felt a hand on my back with a hell of a lot of purpose behind it."

"But who could dislike you so much—" Lillian stood

up. "That's it. I'm calling the police." She gave her niece a stern look. "And don't even think about arguing with me this time. You could have been killed, falling down all those stairs." She picked up the phone and dialed while Jack carefully watched her.

Val glared an *I told you so* at him. Her aunt wouldn't harm a flea. It wasn't in her. More than once in the past, Lillian's good intentions had landed one or both of them in trouble. She wasn't afraid to go out on a limb for loved ones, so it was unthinkable that she would intentionally hurt her niece.

After Grandma had taken her in, Aunt Lillian had visited long and often, bearing marvelous stories and incorrigible fun. Part sister, part aunt, part mother, she had filled a huge void in Val's life. Sure, Lillian was nuts, but it was a loving and lovable nuts. Not a crazed stalker kind of nuts.

Lillian hung up the phone. "They're sending someone over."

"Good." Jack nodded in satisfaction.

"I guess there's no time to change, then." Val grimaced. In the broad light of day, she was feeling grimy and naked under her filthy, mangled dress. She'd never found her bra, and the silky sheath was definitely the worse for wear, given all the bloody gunk they'd applied to it for the party and the weight of the dagger hanging from it all evening. And then there was the fall down the stairs...and the kisses and nearly more on that old couch. She glanced at Jack, then let her gaze slide away. That seemed like days ago. Weeks ago.

Certainly a few accusations and an argument ago.

"Aunt Lillian, could you give me a moment alone with Jack before the police show up?"

Lillian glanced curiously from her niece to Jack. Then, with a secretive, pleased little smile that Val could read with no problem, Lillian nodded. "I'll just be in the kitchen then. I'm watching the news and cleaning up after myself. Yell if you need anything. I'm so glad you're okay."

"Thanks, Aunt Lillian."

After the older woman disappeared into the other room, Val faced Jack down. "Look. I don't know what you plan on telling the police, but don't you dare even mention Aunt Lillian. She didn't push me and she didn't steal all that stuff, *which*—" she raised her brows "—is no longer missing, by the way. It all turned up, just like I said it would."

"Val—"

"Lillian didn't do anything wrong and I won't have her listening to your stupid, groundless accusations and theories."

"They're not groundless. And now I even have something tangible to go on. What'd you do with the blue stuff, anyway?"

Val raised her chin. "I left it in the chest. For Eleanor."

"For a *ghost*? You've got to be kidding me—"

"Val! Jack! Come here! Quickly."

Alarmed, Val hurried off to the kitchen, with Jack hard on her heels. "Aunt Lillian, are you okay?"

"You're not going to believe this!" Lillian stared avidly at the television screen. "They showed the picture, but—"

"Shh." Jack was staring, too.

"...have been collecting evidence and interviewing witnesses and suspects." The television reporter stared somberly from the screen. "Now that they've had a chance to question injured actor Ray Guzmano, they've put out an alert for this woman." The reporter held up a photograph and the camera zoomed in for a better shot. "She's wanted for questioning regarding the assaults on Ray Guzmano and his mother. If anyone's seen or heard from this woman, they should call police at…"

"Holy shit." Jack stared at the TV cameraman's close-up of a professional photograph.

It was a publicity shot—one Valerie knew very well.

"Simone."

AFTER JACK GOT OFF THE PHONE with the police, he turned back to Valerie. "They already have Simone in custody. Her therapist talked her into coming to the police herself."

"Her *therapist*? I didn't know she was even seeing…" Val considered, surprised at first, then not. "Well, it sounds right, actually. Simone in psychotherapy."

"More than you know. She's already been charged with assaults on Mrs. Guzmano and Ray Guzmano. And they were pretty damn interested in the assault on you." He stared at Val. "I told them you wanted to clean up and come by the station later today to give a statement, instead of talking to the officer here. They were okay with that."

Val licked her lips, trying to adjust. "So. This is it then? My cheerful stalker? The person who shoved me down the stairs?" She held out a hand to Jack. "It's Simone?"

He squeezed her hand. "She hasn't been tried yet, but it sure looks that way. No official confirmation of this yet, either, but apparently our friend Simone has been stalking Guzmano, too. For almost three years now. She sent him naked pictures of herself, crazed letters, even posed as his live-in girlfriend a couple times."

"You're kidding."

"No charges were ever filed against her, but that was mostly out of pity, from what I understand." Jack frowned thoughtfully. "Anyway, it explains why her record's clean."

"Scary." Val shook her head. It was all so hard to digest. "And she started this craziness three years ago?"

"Why? Something significant about that time period?"

"It was just a little over three years ago that I was hired on by the network. To play opposite Ray. We started dating soon after. I know he got some disturbing fan mail, but so many actors do that I didn't pay it much attention."

Jack nodded.

Val thought about it some more. "I still don't get it, though. The timing seems off. Those notes didn't start arriving until recently and there was nothing before then. I mean, I could picture a three-year buildup leading to assaults on the Guzmanos, but why didn't she come after *me* three years ago? Why wait until now, when I'm not even seeing Ray?"

Jack shrugged. "Who knows?"

"Well, *she* does. I need to talk to her, Jack. I want to know why she did this."

"Later." Jack gave her a stern look. "First, we get a doctor to check you out. No arguments."

The emergency room doctors gave her a reasonably clean bill of health—bumps and bruises but no fractures or concussion. Jack and Val's subsequent visit to the police station proved less successful. Val wasn't allowed to see Simone, who, they were told, was pleading innocent to all charges and posting bail.

Val gave police a brief statement describing the attack itself and her relationships with Simone and Ray. The detective in charge, who was unavailable, would question her later.

Home again, Val found she could barely keep her eyes open long enough to undress and fall into bed. She was distantly aware of Jack's constant attention and concern. She was grateful for it and wished like hell she was conscious enough to respond in kind. But she was out cold as soon as her head hit the real, honest-to-God pillow.

When she woke the next morning, she was alone in bed, but she could tell by the dents in her pillows and mattress that Jack had lain close to her through the night. Possibly held her, too, given the crick in her neck. Was it pathetic to be jealous of herself? Too bad she hadn't been awake.

Ah, but today she had a full night's sleep behind her and a green light from the doctor. A few bumps and bruises wouldn't stand in her way. On that wicked thought, she showered and dressed with care. Absently, she opened her jewelry box to choose some earrings— She stopped and stared. Lying carefully in their own special velvet-lined compartments were the cameo and the sapphire necklace. Val smiled. "Thanks, Eleanor."

Ten minutes later, she made her way to the kitchen for breakfast. Her aunt and Jack spoke in quiet, heated voices, but just as she entered the room, all conversation ceased.

Jack helped her into a chair. "How are you feeling, honey?"

"Like I fell down a flight of stairs. Shower helped, though. Why? What's going on?" She glanced between Jack and Lillian. "You know, for a mystery writer and a detective, you both have really sucky poker faces. Spill it. What's happened and why am I not going to like it?"

They exchanged looks, then Jack swiped the local paper off the table and handed it to Valerie.

She skimmed it before focusing on an article about a whodunit come to life. "Oh, no. Surely they wouldn't know about—" She cringed. The article told about the food poisoning—like the general public *needed* to be reminded of that, thanks—as well as the notes, the party and the probable reason for it, ending with her fall down the stairs. "Who *is* this reporter and how would he know all this?"

"These journalists have their ways, honey. They could have interviewed some of your help, downloaded information on you and your employees from the Internet, gone through your trash...you name it. I swear I didn't say anything to reporters or the police about the notes or the other stuff, though, Val."

"I believe you." She frowned at the article. "I guess my statement's a matter of public record by now, right?"

He nodded. "That's probably how the reporter got wind of it. They routinely check those things."

Val groaned quietly and Jack just rubbed her shoulder. Finally, she straightened, tried on a game little smile and shrugged. "I guess we'll see where the chips fall, won't we?"

"There's my little fighter." He gave her a teasing look intended to goad her into action.

Val narrowed her eyes, all set to give him exactly what he was provoking, when the phone rang. In fact, the phone rang and rang and rang again—all day long.

Thanks to the article, Longstreet Inn was thriving.

At four o'clock that afternoon, Val cried uncle and switched her phone over to voice mail, before turning, giggling, to Lillian and Jack. "Oh, my God! I couldn't have planned this better myself. People aren't avoiding my inn at all. No, they want to come and *gawk* at the whodunit mystery theater's own stalking victim—and they're willing to pay cash to do it. I'm booked solid for the *next three months!*"

Lillian could hardly contain herself. "Maybe we should take advantage of your popularity and add another matinee during the week? We could even plan a holiday special, with a deranged Santa Claus, maybe? Oooooh." Lillian's eyes gleamed. "And you just *know* there's something funny about all those elves."

Val laughed some more, shaking her head.

Jack watched them with strained patience. "I'm glad you're both so happy about all this. Talk about muddying the investigative waters. Simone hasn't been tried yet, you know."

"Oh, go away, spoilsport. I have work to do. I need to schedule staff and call in food orders and—"

"I get the picture. You'll be busy for a while, right?"

"And then some."

"Good." He frowned at her. "Don't leave. I'm just going into the war room for five minutes to pick up messages."

"Ja-ack. I'm *fine*. Simone's in custody, remember?"

"As far as I'm concerned, your body needs a guard until there's another body convicted and tossed in jail. Got it?"

She grinned. "Wow. Sure. My body would love a guard."

"Tease." But he gave her an amused look. "Don't leave."

"Got it. Freddy and Jason live. Maybe." She waved him away with cheerful impatience. "Be gone with you."

Shaking his head in exasperation, Jack strode off to the war room but left the door open and an eye trained on the hall. Val couldn't leave the inn without walking past him.

And he didn't trust that independent spirit of hers to deny itself should duty or business opportunity beckon.

He quickly dialed his office to pick up messages. Twenty minutes later, he hung up, as shocked as Val had been delighted. There were, indeed, divorces and fretful parents and insurance fraud and suspicious spouses and any number of cases requiring his assistance. Slowly, he headed back to Val's office.

"Can I see that paper again?"

Val looked up, distracted and mildly disgruntled by the interruption. "Paper? There's paper over there."

"*News*paper, Val. I want to see the article."

She blinked, coming back to herself. "Oh." She turned around, grabbed it off a table and handed it to him.

He skimmed the article and, four paragraphs down, found what he thought he might find. So intent had he been earlier on the consequences to Val, that he hadn't even registered the brief mention of his own name in the article. As a local private investigator and consulting expert to Longstreet Inn.

"Problem?" Val gave him a delicately inquiring look.

"Not exactly. Maybe. I'm not sure."

"You're awfully indecisive for a law-enforcement type. What's going on?" She rounded her desk and sat on the couch.

"Business. Is apparently *booming*. Much like yours." He glanced at her. "And for much the same reason."

"Really?" She looked honestly delighted. "Oh, Jack, that's fantastic. Gosh, between your good news and mine, it's almost worth a trip down the steps and a knock on the noggin."

He gave her a repressive look. "Not quite."

"Well, almost. Any plans to sabotage or hurt me have backfired. Right? And we're happy and successful. *We win.*"

"I suppose you could look at it that way."

"You still sound suspicious. Lighten up. It's honest business—people who need your help will get it. All this article did was mention your name and tell them how to find you. It's great publicity, Jack—the lifeblood of any struggling small business."

"Right."

She studied him for a moment then started chuckling. "You know, it's true what they say about you ex-cops and hard-boiled detectives. The only kind of fortune you trust is bad fortune. Good fortune always has an ugly catch. Cynical, cynical, cynical. Why don't you try being simply *grateful*, Jack. Sign up your clients. Solve their cases. Count your cash. It's a *happy* thing."

He grinned, reluctantly.

"That's better. Now come sit with me." She yanked him onto the couch next to her. "I'll rub your poor shoulders. That must have been a stressful half hour for you. Listening to messages from people who want to offer you work and pay you money."

"Smart-ass. You know, I'm still recovering from the sight of your sexy body lying at the bottom of the steps."

"Poor baby. And you haven't had but a tiny little piece of it yet."

"See? Talk about stress."

She chuckled and he tugged her close for a kiss. She was warm and melting against him when he reluctantly pulled back to meet her eyes. "I have something else to tell you. One of my calls was to the police station. If you still want to talk to Simone, I know where we can find her."

Simone, it turned out, was officially released into her mother's custody. Unofficially—and thank God for Jack's connections—Simone's mother and her therapist were trying to talk Simone into a full confession and inpatient therapy. Until the confession or hearing, however, she was under what amounted to house arrest. Her mother, who'd posted bond, didn't trust Simone not to run off when she was in one of her moods.

Jack drove Val to the older neighborhood, and Simone's mother, her eyes pained and wondering, let Val talk privately with her daughter. Not sure what to expect, Val closed the door behind her and let her eyes adjust to the dim interior of Simone's room. "Hello, Simone." Val stared at the disheveled actress, who managed to reek of style, even in a dingy little bedroom.

Simone was sitting on a twin-size bed, flipping through a stack of fashion magazines. "Hello, Miranda." Simone mocked her.

Valerie studied the woman's utterly remorseless gaze. "You really did it, didn't you. You pushed me down the stairs."

"Oh, what to do, what to do. My attorney says to keep my mouth shut, but my therapist says confession's good for the soul. Hmm." She pondered mockingly. "Okay. Sure, I pushed you. I might lie about it later, though." She cocked her head in thought. "Why, I could be lying even now. Maybe I did it, maybe I didn't." Simone's dark eyes gleamed with malicious amusement. "It's true that I don't like you very much, though."

She'd really done it. Simone had shoved her down those stairs. And she'd probably watched, smiling, while Val cartwheeled to the bottom. "But why?"

"You got the part I was supposed to have. Did you know that? I auditioned for Miranda, but you got to be her. Talk about a travesty. I would have made a *wonderful* Miranda." Simone sighed. "And then you had Ray, too, both on camera and off, and you tossed him aside. I wanted Ray, but I couldn't have him. Not even after you were out of the picture. I *still* don't get that part." She looked hurt for a moment.

"So when you didn't get the part, you moved back to St. Louis?" Val tried desperately to keep a chronology going.

"Sure. My mom was here and she was threatening to *tell* people...anyway. But then I found you and, as luck would have it, you needed an actress. It seemed right to take the job from you. But then I wanted Jack, and he wouldn't have a thing to do with me. You got him, too. God. What does it take to get a date with a decent man these days?" She rolled her eyes, obviously considering her explanation complete.

Val bit back a shudder, remembering asking Jack a similar question not so long ago. The dating scene was more of a jungle than she knew, apparently. "So it was after you came on to Jack at the party, and he rejected you. *That's* when you decided to push me down the stairs."

"Yep. Ray and his mom were easier. You took a couple of good, *hard* shoves before you fell. Sure made a lot of noise going down, though." Simone grinned, almost nostalgically.

"Yeah, all that banging and screaming. Doesn't it get a little old, though? First Ray. Then his mom. Then me. All down the stairs?"

Simone shrugged. "Another gift. I am mistress of tears and stairs. They say everyone has at least one talent."

Val was certain she was being mocked now. Was Simone insane or just pretending to be?

Simone's face crumpled a little. "Oh, all right. I didn't mean to shove *Ray*. At least, not so that he'd fall down the stairs and hurt himself like that. I was just pissed that he was such a mama's boy he still wouldn't date me. I mean, what thirty-year-old man brings his *mother* with him to film on location in another city? He's a big boy. Leave mama at home."

Insane or not, Simone was right about one thing. Ray Guzmano surrendered to the apron strings every time. The man had no backbone. But that still didn't justify making an accordion of his spine.

"And you know what else?" Simone continued listing her grievances. "I'd swear Mama Guzmano was the reason I lost the part here, too. How is that fair? I was just auditioning for a little walk-on part any idiot could pull off, and they had to give even that to someone else. A little redheaded *nobody*." Simone smiled ferally but her tone, when she continued, was downright friendly. "But then I thought about it for a while, and you know what? I bet the redhead would look darn cute tumbling head over heels down a spiral staircase."

Val stared, her mind wandering marginally hysterical paths.

"Anyway, the stairs were just so effective—Ray was out cold for *days*, you know—that I did it again." She grimaced. "Should have shoved his mother first, though. That's what really bugs me. Why didn't I think of it before? Shove the *mother*, not Ray. Maybe she'd have been out cold long enough that Ray would let them give me the part. See? Planning." She gave Val a frustrated look. "It's all in the planning."

"Never a strong point for you." Val, numb from the revelations, could hardly believe the words came so nonchalantly from her own mouth.

"Oh, you're so right about that." Simone appeared almost normal for a moment. "I hate memorizing lines. I always excelled at improv. Another strength."

That part was also true. Simone was gifted when she wanted to be. "So why did you do all this now? I bombed on the soap, as you suspected I would do. And anything between Ray and me was over almost three years ago. I know you couldn't have been planning all this for that long. Why would you? And why *me*? Ray dated so many women I don't know how he kept track. I wasn't even with him for very long—haven't seen or heard from him in *years*. But you pushed me, anyway."

Simone shrugged, unconcerned.

"All because of Jack?" Val persisted. "I can't believe you wanted Jack so much, after knowing him such a short time, that you would do all this now and not back then."

"All these questions." Simone gave her an impatient look. "What do you think this is? An elaborate whodunit? *No.* It's really very simple." She continued in a bored singsong. "There was you, there were the stairs, I was close and I knew it could work. What can I say? Opportunity knocked and I opened the door." She chuckled in true delight. "It's not my fault if someone else closed the damn thing after you."

"Someone *else* closed it? What are you saying? You didn't lock me in the basement?"

"Nope. Wish I'd thought of it, though. Talk about dramatic irony." She raised her voice. "Hey, guard. I'm feeling a little fatigued. Could you evict my guest?"

"Simone—"

"Oh, go away. I'm busy." She began tearing at the magazine page again, following the model's profile until the tear went astray and the model lost an appendage. Simone wadded the paper, tossed it across the room and started flipping through the magazine again. "Damn it. Why won't they let me have scissors?"

Footsteps approached and Valerie stood up. "Gee, maybe because you'll stab somebody with them?"

"Oh, please. Do you know how messy that would be? All that blood? The *real* kind? Yuck. It stains, too. Hey, what do you think of this do on me?" Simone turned the magazine so Val could see the model's hairdo. "Cute?" It looked a lot like Val's hair when she played in the soap opera.

"Yeah. Just adorable," Val murmured as Simone's mother opened the door and peered inside.

Sliding a lock of her own hair between two fingers, measuring, estimating, Simone glared at the picture. "I wish they'd give me my scissors back."

"NUTS, BONKERS, rabbits loose in the attic, a house shy of a full deck? She was all of that." Val felt both sad and unnerved as she finished relating her experience to Jack and Lillian. She dropped down into her chair and faced them across her desk. "Simone's crazy. Or maybe putting on a very good act. But I think she's just sincerely nuts."

Lillian frowned. "Simone right under our nose and utterly insane. I suppose it's a marvelous thing that people continue to amaze me, but…" Lillian just shook her head and drifted off, her eyes already glazing over. Plotting. Always plotting. Val smiled as her aunt meandered dreamily out of the office.

"And to think, bunny brain could have been my girlfriend," Jack marveled facetiously after Lillian was out of earshot.

Val widened her eyes, equally facetious. "Yeah. To *think*."

"I'm just glad your aunt wasn't the one behind all this."

"I know. One thing still bugs me, though. Simone swears she didn't close the door after I fell. She didn't lock us in the basement together."

Jack nodded slowly. "I suppose the door was closed behind us by accident?"

Val shrugged, allowing the possibility. "With the party noise and crowds of people...sure. The lock engages automatically when the door shuts. It's a mechanism I had installed when I opened this place up to the public."

"So anyone could have closed it innocently. That's all it would take."

"And, as Simone her bunny self pointed out, this isn't one of our whodunit performances where everything's tidied up and explained away at the end. Jack, I still can't believe it. She shoved me down the stairs on a *whim*. Because it worked with Ray and his mom and because the opportunity presented itself when she was in the right mood. So much for adequate motive and catalyst."

Jack grimaced. "People are complicated. A lot goes on in the human mind—especially the crazed human mind—that we don't know."

"At least *that* wacko mind is off the streets." Val scowled.

"Yep." Jack stood up and approached her, his lips curving.

"What?" She gave him a skeptical look.

"Just this." He touched his lips to hers.

"Mmm." She relaxed and smiled. "Nice. But is that all?"

"Of course not." He kissed her again. "The waiting. It's been driving me insane."

"Really? I *like* that." She stood up and back-walked him until he bumped up against the half-open door, firmly shutting it. She locked it behind him, then tugged him down next to her on the leather couch.

"Hell, yeah. A raving lunatic. You think Simone's bonkers? Just give me one more day of wanting you and having to keep my hands off your sore body." Jack groaned into her lips before taking them hungrily. "Man, I love this dysfunctional stuff."

She laughed as he buried his face in her neck to press glancing kisses at her pulse point and behind her ear. Then he slid lower to nip at the tendon joining neck and shoulder. She flinched. *"Jack."* It was a protest. The teasing little pecks were sending her nerves into a tingling frenzy.

"Oh, you've been teasing me for weeks. Months, even. It's *my* turn." He slid a hand up to her breast, circling and toying with a peak until she gasped and pressed urgently closer. At her shameless response, he grinned, those hazel eyes of his gleaming pure outrageousness. "Hey, check that out. No dead bodies in *this* room."

"Not *yet*, anyway." She narrowed her eyes, promising retribution. "Isn't there something you should be doing here?"

He chuckled against her neck, pulling her closer to rub his cheek against her breast. Nimble fingers she remembered very well deftly unbuttoned the front of her silk dress. "No bra?"

"Nope. It's still missing." She managed a distracted

grin. "Eleanor's keepsake. For her honeymoon, maybe. Remember? Anyway, it's the only one that matches..." She glanced briefly down toward her own panty level.

"*Really.*" His whisper was hot with interest. "So what exactly would go with that pretty little blue bra?" His gaze on her nipple, he stroked gently around it, sending inquisitive fingers seeking the sensitive underside of her breast. He drew closer, letting her feel his breath on her skin. She flinched. "Such a lacy, racy little number, if I remember correctly."

With no warning, he took the peak deep into his mouth. She gasped and went fluid at the feel of his tongue, lips, rasp of teeth against her. Maybe she could melt right down his body and pool in a hormonal, adoring mess around his feet— "Jack." She breathed the word, every part of her shaky with nerves and arousal.

He just grinned, his mouth against her other breast and his hand—stealthy hand, *ho*, boy, nimble-as-*all*-hell fingers—encroaching on her hem, her hose-clad thighs, her lacy blue garter *clip* and...slowed.

She panted, annoyed and aroused at the same time. "Hey, the garter was *mine*. I was going to tease you. To *death*."

"So I see." He peered up at her through his lashes. His fingertips coasted the edge of her stocking, now freed unceremoniously from its dainty moorings. She could hardly breathe. His *pacing*. So unexpected. It was completely unnerving.

Trembling like this, she never would have had the strength to perform that skanky little striptease she'd rehearsed in front of the mirror earlier. To teasingly undo the garter as she'd planned, and carefully roll down the stocking, her body poised just so. She'd watched the reflection of her own eyes, momentarily pretended it was his hot gaze watching her fingers slide down her bared thigh.

She met his eyes now, saw the knowledge of it there—of what she'd planned, of even her preparations—and was as turned on by it as he was. Oh, that he could even suspect, much less visualize. But he knew her. Deep-down knew her. He knew she'd rehearse something as important as the careful, complicated seduction of one Jack Harrison.

The mutual knowledge left her shakier than before. Especially now that she realized how carefully he'd turned the tables on her. So much for rehearsal. She was dealing with the unknown, the untried. It was both thrilling and terrifying.

"You should be illegal, Jack."

He gently traced the edges of his teeth along her ribs, making her flinch. She felt like one long, exposed nerve ending, and he played delicately, wickedly all over her until she was panting and mindlessly craving more.

"My lovely vamp. You were going to seduce me." His words rumbled against her belly, his whiskered throat vibrating against her silk-clad pelvis. "You and these pretty blue garters." He tugged relentlessly at her skirt. "And... *wow*. Lacy thong?"

"Yes," she hissed the single word—couldn't manage anything with actual voice behind it.

"Damn." He groaned. "I'll bet you're good at it, too."

"You bet I am." Her attempt at a saucy smile was spoiled by a silent shriek. Jack was nibbling on the jut of her hip.

"I'll have to let you seduce me, then. *Next* time."

He lowered his hungry mouth to blue lace and a few minutes later, she really did scream, over and over, as she came so hard she jackknifed up. Then she fell, bonelessly, to leather cushions. He pressed gentle kisses to moistened lace, the crease of her thigh. She protested weakly, laughing and flinching from sensitivity, and dragged him up the length of her body.

"Val." He whispered it tensely against her neck, tracing kisses up it until he nipped and drew hungrily at her lip. "I want you so bad, but—"

She pulled back. "But *nothing*." She raised her voice in outrage. "You're *stopping*?"

"Only for now. No condom, baby." He groaned it, burying his face in her neck, his hips restless against her. "Smooth, eh?"

"I'm good if you're good," she mumbled. "Pill. Healthy."

"I've been almost a damn *monk* since— Yeah, I'm healthy. Okay. You're okay?"

"Shut up and come here." She tugged at his belt, wrestled impatiently with it, to his curses and winces. Finally, a manic look in his eyes, he held her off.

"Damn it, Val. Contrary to popular belief, I only have one. If you yank it off, I can't *do* anything with it—"

She shrieked with outraged laughter, nearly wept with it, and he was grinning as he managed to kick off pants and boxers.

Still laughing and growing hungry for him again, she tugged him close, up and *in*. They moaned in unison, rocking hips together in a rhythm so full of relief, Val really did feel tears slipping down her cheeks. "I feel like I've wanted you forever, Jack," she whispered against his skin, feeling his kisses along her temple, her eyelid, her ear. "It's only been weeks. Months, maybe. But *forever*."

"Me, too, babe. Me, too."

"But, *boy*, were you worth the wait." It was a heartfelt

declaration. With a breathless laugh, Jack tipped her hips up and drove deep, proving he had yet more moves—and her oversensitized flesh couldn't take it. She came again, trembling and gasping, while he thrust hard and fast and surrendered to his own release.

Rubbery bones and happy, happy little hearts required that they lay there, just like that, intertwined and letting their breathing slow in syncopation. Val had never felt closer to a human being and it was scary as hell. But, oddly enough, she was in the mood for more self-induced fear.

"Jack."

"Hmm?"

"I could fall...really, *really* hard for you. If I let myself." She took a deep breath and let it out. She could say more, but no *way* was she saying the *L* word before he did. She needed to give him this much, but Mr. Cynical Detective could make the big declaration first, thanks. *She'd* been throwing herself at *him* for eons. It was *his* turn to trust *her*. "So there you have it. No act, just me. It's what you wanted, right?"

His eyes darkened and he took her mouth in a long, soul-plundering kiss. She could hardly keep up. He was so fierce, his hold on her so tight, as he tugged her up and onto his lap to deepen a kiss that already overwhelmed her. He pulled back, but only far enough to study her, hard, as though looking for something. A catch?

"Jack?"

"You're going to take it back."

"No, I'm not." She scowled. "I am, however, demanding some kind of response. More than just a tongue in my mouth."

His lips twitched and he touched his forehead to hers.

"Well?" She moved her head away.

"Well what? I'm human. Give me some recovery time and we'll go a second round."

"You are *such* a man." She groaned in frustration. "*Talk*, damn it. Tell me. Something. *Anything*. I'm not proud. Well, I used to be, but obviously I'm not anymore. Just what *is* it about a man that wrings every last drop of pride from a woman, anyway? *You're* the one who insisted I drop any act or game or whatever and just be myself. Well, there I go, be myself, and I get sex, which is what I wanted. But I was sort of expecting that you wanted to offer more..." She continued grumbling until he tipped her chin up.

"What do you want me to say? That you fascinate me? That you enthrall me, bewitch me, amuse me, frustrate the *hell* out of me? That you twist my heart and stomach into knots every *damn* time I see you?" Hazel eyes glittered with warring emotion.

She stared, stunned nearly speechless. "Um. Yeah, that'll work. Sure." Hell, she was breathless again. No, he hadn't mentioned the *L* word in that long, passionate spiel, but he'd certainly growled all the other ones at her.

"Good. Too *damn* bad for me that every word of it's true."

He sounded so disgruntled she couldn't help but laugh and mock just a little. "You sound mad about it, too."

He gave her a harassed look. "I am. It feels like I just willingly stuck my head through a choke collar and leash."

Miffed at the comparison, she tried to tug free of him.

He didn't relax his hold on her, but his chest shook with silent laughter. "Not that I'd do that for any other woman, you understand."

"Gee. How flattering." But she stopped resisting.

He kissed her temple. "Cut me some slack, lady. My last

girlfriend screwed up my career and sent my father into early retirement. And I was only attracted to her, when I'm damn near nuts about you." He laughed. "I'm thinking you could be lethal."

She wanted to grin like an idiot but fought desperately for a lighter, teasing tone. "You just keep talking about ex-girlfriends, and I'll show you lethal."

"MAIL TIME." Lillian cheerfully breezed into the office the next day. Patting her hair, she found her glasses and plucked them out to slide carefully onto her nose. "Let's see now." She flipped through the envelopes. "We have bills…bills…"

"…more bills…" Val cheerfully supplied.

"…ads…personal mail…?" Lillian gave Val a curious look and handed her a parchment-colored envelope.

Val winced. Not again. "Is it from jail, by any chance?"

It was the usual standard-size envelope but stuffed to the point of no longer being flat. Lillian turned it over, exposing a heavily taped exterior.

"Nope. Actually, there's no postmark or address. This was hand delivered. And your name's scribbled on it. Strange."

Val moaned. "Not again."

"I'll go get Jack."

JACK CAREFULLY SLIT the end of the bulky envelope. It gapped open to reveal a swatch of blue lace.

Feeling suddenly queasy, Val met Jack's eyes. "That's…"

"Yeah, I know."

"What?" Impatient, Lillian snatched the swatch from

the envelope. "A *bra*? Who would send you a bra, Valerie? Maybe that wicked Simone with something twisted up her sleeve. Or maybe that nasty Phyllis Burlington commenting on propriety or—"

"No. The bra is mine." Val grabbed it and wadded it into an unrecognizable blue puff. It was the same bra she'd lost when she and Jack were locked in the basement.

She didn't know what was more humiliating. Having her bra on display for aunt, lover and whichever pervert had crammed it into an envelope. Or knowing her cup size was small enough that it actually *fit* inside an envelope.

Lillian looked appalled. "You mean someone stole your *underwear*?" Then, glancing from Val to Jack and back again, her eyes widened outrageously. "Oh. Oops. Look, if I've spoiled some sort of kinky *game* you two are playing…" She blinked, that plotting look glazing her eyes over again. "Although it is interesting, just from a spectator's vantage point. I thought the idea was to pretend a fantasy that's *different* from your everyday life, which lately has resembled fatal attraction and stalking and this would be *just* like— But who am I to judge? I'll just pretend I never saw this."

"We're not—" Val sighed. "Look, the bra's been missing. I lost it that night we were locked in the basement." Val met Jack's eyes, remembering nimble fingers undoing and slipping the garment right off her body. Along with shame, inhibitions and any defenses she might have constructed around her heart. He'd gotten past all of them. A lousy bra was no hindrance. Her gaze softened, as did her knees. Jack smiled just a little before sobering and returning his attention to the envelope.

Lillian was studying the wadded-up bra in Val's hand.

"I just had a thought. You said you lost your brassiere in the basement. And it *is* blue." She raised an eyebrow at her niece. "Do you suppose…?"

"The bride? Oh, no. Sure, a lot of blue things around here disappear and then reappear, but not once has the ghost dropped something into an envelope and taped it shut to be delivered with the mail. No, a person did this. The question is why."

Jack turned over the envelope. Valerie watched him trace a finger over a familiar crease at the top. Although weakened by the bulk of the envelope's contents, that crease made this envelope a match for the others. "I'm more curious about *who*."

"I thought it was over, Jack."

"Apparently not. Let me call for an update on Simone's case, see what else I can find. I'll catch up to you later."

She groaned. "So much for closure."

"WE NEED TO TALK." Jack spoke from the doorway to her office. His face was unreadable, his voice flat.

"That doesn't sound good." Val dropped her pen back on her desk.

"It doesn't, does it. Meet me in the library. Ten minutes." He turned and strode off.

11

LESS THAN TWENTY MINUTES LATER, four people gathered in the war room: two women and two men, facing each other from opposite sides of the table. It wasn't exactly the setting and tone Val had envisioned, but apparently this was no production of hers. She stared at Jack, uneasy now. He looked pretty damn distant for a man who'd just made love with her less than twenty-four hours ago.

Jack, who sat next to his father and across from Val and her aunt, straightened in his chair and spoke evenly. "I talked to the police detective handling the assaults on the Guzmanos and on Valerie. He said Simone came in to the station yesterday and confessed to all three attacks."

"Simone *confessed*?" Val stared. Wow.

"To everything involving the Guzmanos, and to the assault on you." Jack eyed Val. "But she denies sending anonymous notes to me or to you. Threatening or otherwise."

"And you believe her?" Val studied his darkened features.

"I think she'd get herself off a little easier if there weren't notes proving premeditation, but I'm inclined to believe her. She confessed to everything involving the Guzmanos. I think she'd be happy to brag about your notes, too. If she sent them."

Lillian gazed at him thoughtfully. "So you brought us here to try to solve your case?"

He raised an eyebrow. "I guess you could see it that way."

Lillian smiled. "Why, Detective. Are you implying more?"

"Maybe I am. I've been weighing just who had the most to gain from this whole business." He turned to Valerie.

Val blinked at him. "To gain from what business?"

"Notes that invited publicity and resulted in profit."

"Profit. I see." No, she didn't. God, she *hoped* she didn't. He couldn't mean—

Jack continued in a voice devoid of all emotion. Paired with his shadowed features, which revealed not a damn thing to her, that tone sent shivers down Val's spine. "If we look at the facts, Val, it seems to me that you had motive, opportunity and, together with your aunt's expertise, a hell of a lot of means. Who else could produce a convincing sham of a crime but the experts on fiction and crime?"

"Jack, darling, don't you think you're stretching matters just a little?" Lillian tried a coaxing smile. "Honestly—"

"Lillian, just stop before you dig yourself in any deeper." Jack's father gave her a shaming look. "I told Jack where I found that envelope I used to mail back Valerie's…ahem."

"*You* mailed it to me? But how did you get it?" Puzzle pieces clicked halfway into place. "Wait a minute. *You're* the boyfriend. The guy my aunt's been dating."

Robert glanced at his son, then, reddening, at Lillian. "Yes, I've been seeing your aunt. Discreetly." He mumbled the rest. "I helped install security, remember. So, with your aunt's permission and to avoid causing talk, I often let myself in through the basement. Jack damn near caught me at it that first time I tried it, too. He thought I was a prowler. Anyway, that's why the key was missing. It's also where I found the..." He reddened again then cleared his throat with a half-angry cough. "Anyway, I also showed Jack the stack of old wedding invitations your aunt kept in her drawer next to those envelopes."

Lillian frowned in obvious surprise. "*You* did?"

"What wedding invitations?" Val gave her aunt a baffled look. "You were married?"

Jack answered for her. "Invitations to a wedding between Lillian and your *father*. The wedding never took place but, coincidentally enough, the date of the planned wedding was October 2. Ring a bell, Val?"

"The date of my supposed funeral." She stared, her breath caught in her throat, at Jack, his father, her own *aunt*? She didn't know what to think. Did she know any of these people?

The elder Harrison looked stubborn now. "That's right. And that stack of wedding invitations was sitting in a drawer of Lillian's desk, right next to a stack of parchment-colored envelopes with a distinctive crease at the top of them. Incriminating as hell." He glowered at his lover. "Damn it, Lillian. Just what were you trying to accomplish?"

Lillian had a faraway look in her eyes. "*Oh*. Such melodrama. I've been exposed by my secret lover."

"Lillian!" Val squeaked the word through a tight throat. She couldn't believe— "*You* wrote those threats and sent them to me? How *could* you?"

The amusement faded from Lillian's face and she frowned at her niece. "Oh, darling. They weren't intended to hurt you." She raised her nose and looked down it reprovingly. "In fact, they might have actually *helped* if you'd just played this thing out like you were supposed to."

"Helped? Threatening to hurt me would actually *help* me?"

"Oh, for heaven's sake, you don't think I'd actually hurt you, do you?"

The tightness eased fractionally. "Well, I didn't used to think so, but—"

"But *nothing*. No, indeed. We were gaining all this nice publicity, and people were starting to pay you attention, and soon they'd be paying my writing attention. We'd have been rich and famous in no time." She patted her hair. "Why, those publishers in New York might have wanted to buy my stories. I could be the next Agatha Christie, if someone would just recognize my talent."

Valerie wondered if her own aunt had gone nuts. The world was peopled with rabbits. "You did this to gain attention for your *writing*?"

Lillian stiffened in mild affront. "Well, only *partly*. I wanted your business to be a success. And then there was Jack Harrison, too. He was perfect for you, but neither one of you could see it." She smiled. "You see it now, though, don't you. I managed to throw the two of you together often enough that you finally saw past your problems and fell in love. Just like you were meant to do. See? All nice and tidy."

"But—" Val shook her head. "The note in Jack's car suggested he stay *away* from me. That's not matchmaking."

Lillian chuckled wickedly. "Of course it is, darling. A little helping of reverse psychology, add a dash of the tempting forbidden…and, oh, my, did that spice things up."

Val stared, speechless with shock and embarrassment.

"So explain the date, then. Why?" Jack's voice was hard.

Lillian sighed, obviously lost in nostalgia. "The second

of October. The date I might have married Valerie's father." Her smile was poignant. "Oh, not that I really wanted to marry him. He was a bit of a stick-in-the-mud, if you want the truth. No offense, Val. But you, darling, I always looked upon you as the daughter I might have had, if only... So you could say I chose the date out of sentiment. And for lovers' luck." She glanced craftily from her niece to an unsmiling Jack.

"Oh, Aunt Lillian, I love you, too." It was touching. *Really.* "But *death* threats? What if I had gone to the police?"

The older woman tipped her head forward, her eyes pitying. "Valerie, really. You know the police wouldn't have done anything but file a report for you. Besides, I counted on your business sense to keep everything under wraps."

"I...really don't know what to say. I'm shocked."

"And what about locking us in the basement? And I'm not buying the door accidentally closing, either," Jack said. "Not with as much manipulation as I've seen so far."

"Guilty again. That was me. Just, well, matchmaking again. But I unlocked it the next day."

Jack looked furious now. "What if Valerie had been seriously injured when she fell down those stairs?"

"Honestly, I didn't know she'd fallen." Lillian's expression was troubled. "I just heard voices—yours and hers—and closed the door on you. I thought a little time alone together would give you an opportunity to work out your differences and reconnect." She paused. "And see? I was right."

Ignoring that last part, Jack continued to press her. "What about leaking that story to the press? Was that you, too?"

"No, I'm afraid not."

"Profitable, though, now wasn't it." Jack swung his gaze to Valerie. "You, perhaps? To gain publicity for the inn? Hell, why not? No harm, no foul, right? Once word gets out that the much-publicized stalking is a farce, you'll both be such a hit—whodunit experts who stumped even the detective—that everyone will just laugh about it. Especially at the *idiot detective who doesn't solve the case.*"

"Jack—"

"Just how many new reservations *have* you booked since the stalking started and that story ran in the newspaper?"

Val crossed her legs and regarded him coolly, her heart sinking. "Dozens, easily. And I expect more." She raised her chin. "I can't help what people think. What lures them."

"No, but you can damn sure make money off of it, can't you." His voice was cold. "What an excellent PR scam. Engineered so craftily by your aunt and personal scriptwriter. So which parts did you concoct, Val? Any personal favorites? How about the one where the detective looks like an ass in public for not identifying the real criminal or revealing the scam?"

"Why do you even bother to ask?" Val spoke with quiet certainty. "You don't give a damn what really happened. You don't want the truth. You just want to know what the hell you can blame me for. So you can validate every doubt you ever had about me. You never did trust me, did you?"

He didn't answer.

"You think I planned this, or at least part of it. To make money. And to make a fool of you." She regarded his expression calmly for a moment, then threw her arms wide and forced a painfully dazzling smile. "Well, *hey*, you found me out. You must be one helluva P.I. Yep, that was me.

"Oh, and Simone and Aunt Lillian making confessions?" She feigned a crazed look with a triumphant grin to go with it. "No, they're really just *plants*. To throw you off the real culprit. *Me*. I really did everything myself. Wrote nasty little notes to myself, told the press every sordid detail of the happenings here at my inn—my *home*—and then I *even* kicked my *own* ass down the steps and managed to lock the door behind me as I fell. See? Not only am I a Broadway-caliber actress—it's the only reason I could pull this off, you know—but I'm also *amazingly* double-jointed. Just makes you pant, doesn't it?

"Oh, and let's not forget spiteful sociopath. I did, after all, engineer all of this *just* to make you look bad." The smile really hurt but wasn't leaving her damn face now. "And it would have worked so well if you hadn't found me out. Oooooooh, foiled again." The performance would have been a lot more effective if it hadn't ended on a shrill, broken note, but a girl could only expect so much, right?

"Val—"

"Feels lovely being right, doesn't it, Jack? All that talk about trust and opening up is just bullshit, isn't it. I trusted you, but you couldn't find it in yourself to trust me."

She bit down on her lip, trying to hold back tears. The uncertainty in his eyes was playing hell with her composure. "Get the hell out of my inn and stay away from me." She turned and walked out of the room.

When Jack made as if to follow her, Lillian blocked his path and smiled calmly. "If you want to know who leaked the story to the press, why, my money's on Phyllis Burlington."

He gave her an annoyed, distracted look. "The reviewer?"

"The very one. I saw Simone and Henri talking to her at the party, probably feeding the woman's passion for gossip." Lillian raised an eyebrow pointedly. "And, unless I misinterpreted her glares, the woman seems to have taken a personal dislike to *you*. Was it something you said, darling?"

Jack scowled and tried to walk around Lillian, but she gracefully sashayed back into his path. "And, obviously, Phyllis has the connections and temperament to get a story like that printed. Valerie, with her loyal little heart, has too much class for that." She shook her head. "You know, I've tried to capitalize on that business sense of hers, but she just won't cross certain lines."

Valerie, who took complete advantage of her aunt's interference, strode quickly, purposefully to her own room. She refused even to acknowledge the tears that wanted to spill over so bad she could taste them.

Simone was right. Tears had never been a strong point for her, either onstage or off. There was no dignity in crying. *None*, damn it. Swiping the tears from her cheeks, she kicked the door closed behind her—and wanted to cuss when it swung right back open.

So she did. "*Damn* it. Go away. I don't want you here."

"No. I can't. I'm sorry, Val." Jack spoke in a quiet, raspy voice. "For everything. You're right. I should have trusted you. It's no excuse, but this seemed to come out of nowhere. It threw me. And with your aunt involved and the money to be made and you always defending her so fiercely..." He shrugged.

"So I must be guilty, right? You decided I was guilty before you even talked to me about it. Right from the start you couldn't stand to think I might be anything morally above a common criminal. First I'm guilty of staging a fake stalking, then of defrauding my insurance company and now of profiting from hurting you. I just can't win with you. Why is that?"

"Well…"

Valerie laughed, but it was a choked sound. "Oh, wait. Don't tell me. I'm being punished for your ex-girlfriend, right? The one who betrayed you?"

"I was wrong."

She turned to face him. "You bet your ass you were wrong. On every count. Even if you think nothing of my morals, Jack, do you think a scandal like this is something I'd plan? On some gamble that it would bring in new business? I'd go insane with worry. I *love* this inn. It's mine. My one and only chance to make a success of myself at something I'm really, really good at. Screw you and screw anything we might have had together, but I'd never jeopardize my home. *And* my future. *And* my friends."

And she was a liar. She'd never have hurt *him* like that, either. She loved him too much.

Not that *he* needed to hear that right now. Her dignity and what was left of her stubborn pride protested the very idea. No, she was a complete fool for loving the man. He'd never return her feelings or loyalty. Never trust her enough—love her unconditionally—that she could begin to feel safe with him.

Be yourself, he'd said. *Be real.* Better yet, *be a walking open wound,* just to give him satisfaction. Forget that. Walking open wounds lost out to vamps every day of the week, and she was tired of losing. Especially when it was her heart she lost and to an ex-cop who would only torture it into a false confession.

"I guess I deserved that."

"You certainly did. Now get out." When his stubborn

look forecast a refusal, she glared at him. "Just what would happen to your P.I.'s license if I called the cops and had you forcibly escorted off the premises?" She picked up her phone. When he didn't move, she started dialing.

Jack's eyes flashed frustration, but he backed off a step and reached for the doorknob. "I'll be back. I'm not giving up."

She gave a half laugh. "Hell, Jack, you gave up before we even got started."

12

"So you're through? You and Jack? Don't be a complete *fool*, Valerie Longstreet. It's been almost a week. Forgive the man."

"Aunt Lillian!" Val frowned across her desk at her aunt. They were sitting quietly, sharing coffee and various periodicals. It was their usual early-morning ritual, but for some reason, it just made Val restless. Maybe because she'd imagined different mornings for a while. Another face, perhaps. Smiles and laughing kisses. Sleepy lovemaking at dawn. Was that too much to ask?

Apparently.

"I'm serious, Valerie. I fully support every woman's right to make her man crawl when he's drawn some asinine conclusions. But Jack has groveled exceptionally well, young lady."

"Ha." Val shook out the newspaper and continued reading.

"*Ha?* What about those chocolates? They were *imports*."

"Trite. Good, but trite." She whipped to the next page.

"And the flowers? A beautiful bouquet of mixed orchids and even a little note to go with them. Although, I don't know who he's calling *dysfunctional* or why that would even be desirable."

"I'm allergic to orchids."

"Oh." Lillian straightened in her chair and reached for a fresh magazine. "Well, then, I think you should march right over to his office and tell him so. That's just what he deserves."

"You're being transparent." Val scowled. "He doesn't trust me, Aunt Lillian. That's a little worse than forgetting my birthday. Flowers and chocolates work for that. Not for this. And you're not going to trick me into going over there and dealing with him again, so give it up."

"Hmph. After all my hard work." She flipped the magazine open.

Val gave her aunt a look.

"Well?" Her spine rod-straight, Lillian peered at her niece over her spectacle lenses. "I *did* work hard to get you two together. I took risks. I planned. I schemed."

"You *defrauded*."

"Picky, picky, picky." Lillian studied her for a frowning moment. "So tell me. Besides your hopeless wreck of a love life, the worst part of this fiasco is that Jack's business will suffer once that reporter gets wind of the details behind his latest case. Right?"

Val raised an eyebrow at the "hopeless wreck" part of her aunt's question but let it pass. "That's the part he was throwing in my face, yes. A P.I. fooled into investigating a fake stalking? And who later gets locked up against his will by his quarry? Not exactly positive publicity."

"Ah, youth. So shortsighted." Lillian shook her head. "I was honestly just trying to help you two find each other. You belong together, and, frankly, it worked until you both tripped all over your pride."

"It's not pride, Aunt Lillian. Jack and I don't have a relationship because he doesn't trust me. It has nothing to do with the case. Honestly. I don't blame Jack for being upset about how everything worked out. If anyone's hurt by all this scheming, it's going to be him. I'm fine. You and Jack's dad made up. And Simone will get the help she needed to begin with."

"I suppose you're right. Jack didn't get a fair deal from us, did he?" Lillian frowned.

"No." Val gave her aunt a pointed look.

"I'll figure something out."

"Lillian—"

"Let's talk about trust." Lillian spoke over her niece's alarm and subsequent groan. "If you think about it rationally for a moment, you can hardly blame Jack for that mere moment or two wherein his trust in you faltered."

"Oh, I can blame him."

"Well, you shouldn't. The man's a detective and former cop. Suspicion and mistrust are part of the job description. Not to mention extremely attractive. You've even said so yourself."

"Sure, it's attractive. Unless *I'm* the one he mistrusts. And, for that matter, his job doesn't require him to *assume* I'm guilty. That's worse than just suspecting."

"Oh, lighten up, Val. Nobody's perfect. People will make mistakes and, after a respectable amount of groveling, other people will have to forgive them. I certainly hope *your* groveling works when you need it to. Now as for the rest..." An unfocused intensity washed over her face.

Valerie recognized the look and completely abandoned the newspaper. "*You*. You're plotting. Stop that. Unless it involves only *fictional* circumstances and *fictional* characters, you can just quit that right now."

"Calm down, Valerie. I've learned my lesson." Lillian raised her nose in the air. "I'm just weaving some story threads together. Perhaps a slightly different nuance. Hmm." Lillian smiled serenely. "Why don't you run along so I can work this out. Oh, but before you go, I have a wonderful idea for next month's show. Do you think Mandy would mind using a chain saw?"

"A chain saw." Valerie just stared.

"Yes. Now, I'll admit I've always thought they were too crude for true whodunits. And that most people expect a certain amount of tradition in these stories. You know, the old-fashioned methods. Poison, strangulation, a dueling pistol, that kind of thing. But I'm starting to think we need to keep up with the times a little more. Attract a younger crowd."

"Maybe." Val gave her a wary, half-intrigued look.

"I thought, given Mandy's wholesome, girl-next-door looks, a chain saw might be a poetic addition. Although...a machine gun might be more immediately effective." Lillian frowned thoughtfully. "How would I get my hands on one of those?"

"I think they're illegal." Val regarded her aunt with alarm, afraid legality might not prove a sufficient obstacle....

"Hmm. Yes. I'll have to play with this a little more. Really, Valerie, I do need some privacy. My muse, you know." She shooed Valerie out of her own office and closed the door.

Okay, so maybe her aunt really was stalker-level crazy. Completely bonkers. Thankfully, she wasn't violent. No, Aunt Lillian used her powers of insanity for good, not evil.

A smart niece would be grateful for small favors.

"Here. Read it." Lillian, a triumphant little smile on her face, handed Valerie a tabloid a few days later.

At a loss, Valerie took the latest issue of *Gateway* and read the front-page headline.

Local Detective Solves the "Case"

"Oh. Boy." Dreading what else might befall them, Valerie skimmed the story. She had to go back and reread when her nerves got the best of her, but after a few moments, the gist of the story got through. She looked up, shocked.

Impressed.

"Lillian. You arranged this?"

Lillian shrugged modestly. "Consider it the epilogue to this little drama of ours. I needed one to tie up some loose ends. And I sort of had the lovely but flawed and well-*connected* Phyllis Burlington at my complete disposal, so I simply told her the whole story. In *confidence*, of course. It's the only way to get the woman to print a thing. She's convinced that this will ensure her future as a gossip columnist. I believe that's the first time I've seen that woman look truly joyful."

"You're shameless." Val spoke absently, still skimming the article almost feverishly. "But this was a stroke of genius. This story makes it sound like you and I planned the whole thing. Intentionally. And as a standard, if sneaky, public relations event." Valerie narrowed her eyes. "And that Jack participated wholeheartedly in testing you and me and the inn and the inn's staff.

"It all just sounds…so close to the truth and yet better. Despite her worst intentions, Phyllis Burlington's reporter friend makes Jack look good in this story. Like he was the one who outwitted us and that we were humbly grateful for his tutelage while the professional outwitted the fictional." She stared at Lillian. "Utterly brilliant. You terrify me."

"What can I say? Our detective needed a happy ending. At least of one kind." She gave her niece a pointed look.

"Don't start." Val narrowed her eyes in warning. "He accused me of using him, remember? He walked into that room thinking *I* had planned it all and even had the gall to hire him to investigate what I supposedly *knew* was a sham case. He accused me of *defrauding* him and all of you and the media—"

Her aunt shrugged carelessly. "*I* was guilty of some of that, and you and I are related. It could run in the family."

Val groaned. "Don't say that. I'm already counting on eventual insanity. Let's not add fraud and manipulation to my future prospects."

"Whatever you say, dear. And, now that you've told me exactly how you feel about the subject, you won't hear another peep from me about your sexy detective. Not. A. Peep." While Val steamed silently over the non-peeping peeps, Lillian just smiled at her. "The mail came, dear. There's a stack on your desk."

Mail. She'd take even bills to distract her thoughts from that cynical, accusing, sexy, huge-hearted— She stalked off to her office. Pushing another vase of flowers out of her way—daisies, this time—she flipped mindlessly through the stack until she came to one in particular. And dropped the others. "Lillian!"

"Ye-es?" Lillian peeked around the doorjamb.

"Have you been up to your old tricks again?"

"Now, Val. That sounded *nearly* disrespectful." Lillian quietly entered Val's office. "Are you sure—"

"The *envelope*." Val dangled it in front of her aunt's spectacles.

"Well, *I* didn't send it." Lillian blinked at her. "You know I don't recycle old plotlines."

"Then who did?"

"I dislike stating the obvious, but I suppose you could try opening it to find out."

Annoyed, Val slit the envelope and pulled out a small invitation.

To a memorial service blessing Jack Harrison's cremated remains.

Lillian, reading over Val's shoulder, just met her niece's eyes with a wide-eyed expression. "I didn't send it. I didn't."

"Hmm. You know, these guessing games are just great in fiction. In real life, however, they're getting a little old."

Lillian glanced warily at the invitation and then at Val. "What are you going to do, then?"

"Oh, that's easy enough." Val smiled ferociously. "I'll just kill him myself and be done with it."

WHEN THE OUTER DOOR of his office slammed open with enough force to rattle his teeth, Jack decided he had his answer.

"Jack Harrison. How dare you mock me. After *everything*."

Nope. Not even laughing on the inside.

But she was *here* and she was speaking to him—which was further than he'd gotten in days, even weeks now. This was good.

Although, when she blazed into his office mere seconds later, he had cause to reconsider. The woman wasn't just unjoyful; she was downright pissed.

Strike pissed. Make that hostile. Volatile. He was a dead man walking. *Sitting*. Whatever. "Val, I—"

"Nope. *There* you are. Alive and breathing. Such a damn shame." She flipped the memorial invitation onto his desk. "It's really unkind to get a girl's hopes up like that and not—" She stopped and stared as he rose to his feet. "What's going on?"

Jack's office—normally a sparsely furnished cubicle-looking place, for all the building's natural beauty—had been rendered almost romantic, with soft jazz playing and a candelabra fluttering quietly by the window. With the cloudy gloom of late afternoon beyond the window, the candles cast an intimate glow in the small room.

Jack gave her a lopsided grin. "I'm just testing out a little theory."

"A *theory*? About me, I suppose."

"Well, I know you have this affinity for dead bodies, so I thought this was one sure way of getting you here. The promise of *my* dead body. And see? It worked."

She choked, her soft, brown eyes bugging just a little. "That's. *Sick*."

"A little dysfunctional maybe?"

"Or a *lot*."

"So I'm on the right track." Jack had dressed in a casket-appropriate suit and tie with a matching silk handkerchief folded in his pocket. He stepped quietly toward her. "Any chance I could get you to do the makeup?"

Her eyes widened and she pressed her lips together, but a snort of laughter escaped, anyway.

"I understand you do great dead people. Great or not, I'm more than willing to give it a try. Wanna do this dead body?"

She couldn't even hold back the giggles this time. "Oh, Jack. That's really horrible."

He chuckled. "I learned from the best."

"Yeah?" Suddenly, Val looked vulnerable, and his own smile faded.

"Maybe not very well. Yet. I am new at this dysfunctional stuff, after all. But I'm also a quick learner. I'm excellent at research. Adaptable. Hell, I just switched careers a couple of years ago, and now I can find ditzy poodles even on a bad day. Surely I can learn something as basic as trust. In someone as genuine and gutsy as you."

"Oh, Jack." But she was wavering. He could see it. "Why was it so hard for you to trust me? Every time I turned around you suspected me of something."

"It's that whole emotion bit."

"'Emotion bit.' Right." She scowled. "What kind of line is that?"

"Okay, okay. I'm trying." He paused to gather his thoughts. "It's like this. I'm a cop. Or I used to be. Automatic suspicion's just part of the job. It's part of a P.I.'s job, too."

"Oh, come on, Jack. You didn't just look at me with ordinary suspicion. That implies you give a person a chance to defend herself or himself. That innocence is still a possibility. You just *assumed* I was guilty from the first."

"You're right. I was wrong. I guess...when my emotions—hell, *anyone's* emotions—are involved, I have a hard time trusting people. I've seen too many cases where people betray the ones they love and the ones who love them. That's why, when a woman is killed, cops always look first to husbands and boyfriends. Odds are, they're the ones who murdered her."

She stared at him as though trying to rearrange nonsense into sense. "So you're telling me you made those idiotic assumptions about me because you *cared*?"

"Could be it's my own special way of saying I love you?" He tried a grin. "Twisted, huh? Almost...*dysfunctional*, even."

"Oh, Jack. If that weren't so sweet, it would be pathetic."

"I know. Val, I'm so sorry. For every stupid thing I thought and said about you that day. I guess I considered it a preemptive strike. It was just so damn hard to believe in someone as uniquely *Valerie*...as you. There had to be a catch. And there I was head over heels, crazy in love with you. It was so hard to believe that you might feel the same for me."

He smiled. "But here I am. Laying it all on the line for you—and without even knowing how you feel. That's trust, right? *I love you*. And I mean *all* of you, Val. The woman who loves to tease and vamp it up while she's giggling at me with those expressive eyes. The one who's mad enough to be homicidal except her soft heart would never, ever let it go that far."

"Oh, I wouldn't count on that—" She tried to interject.

He grinned appreciatively. "I would. Otherwise, I'd be dead by now. You were mad as hell at me."

"You're right. I was furious." She approached him with silken grace, her eyelashes sweeping low. "That means I owe you a dead body, don't I. So. Makeup, huh? But that invitation said you went up in flames, Detective."

He swallowed hard. "Well. I had this really hot dream the other night. Haven't slept a wink since then..."

She smiled. "*Really*. And who set the fire?"

"Do you even have to ask." He tugged her, laughing, into his arms. "Damn, but I've missed you. Everyone else around me is so *sane* I can't stomach it."

"So you need a little dysfunctional wack in your day-to-day life, do you?"

"You have something in mind?"

"Of course. I love you, too. So, Jack Harrison, you're going to *marry* me and all my dysfunctionality."

He gave her a knowing look. "Marriage, huh? Oh, that's sneaky. You're just trying to get out of paying my finder's fee."

"*What?*" There was true outrage in her eyes. "What finder's fee? I don't owe you any *finder's* fee."

"I found your stalker, didn't I?"

"*No-o!*"

"Then who did?" He raised a challenging eyebrow.

She gave him a disgruntled look. "Simone confessed, your dad busted my aunt and my aunt cleared me. And *I* had to find my own sapphires. Looks to me like your case was solved by everyone *except* you. So you can just stop—"

"See? I *need* wack in my life. You're good for me."

"—insulting my business sense and—*mmph.*"

He took her mouth, and after a moment, she softened and her lips curved up to match his. "Jack."

"Yes, I'll marry you."

"Good. My aunt can plan the wedding."

"God help us all."

"CAN WE GO NOW?" An impatient male complained in a stage whisper. Voices rose in laughter and protest beyond the door he was pressed against. "I just heard something about seduction and whose turn it might be—and I damn well *know* my son doesn't want anyone listening in on that."

"Robert, hush just a minute." A female snapped at him without raising her ear from the wooden portal. "I'm planning the wedding, did you hear? I want to hear if they set a date. Halloween would be perfect—"

"Honey, they will set a date, and when they do, we'll be the first to know."

"Yes, but—"

"It's *their* decision. Come on, Lillian. Let's go back to your place." His rasping whisper lowered to a coaxing thread of sound. "I bought some blue boxers the other day. I thought we could go in through the basement and run a little investigation of our own..."

Whispers mingled with low laughter and the scene faded to a soft, happy glow.

HARLEQUIN ROMANCE

Introducing Southern Cross Ranch, a three-book miniseries by Harlequin Romance favorite **Barbara Hannay**

Southern Cross Ranch

Family secrets, Outback marriages!

Deep in the heart of the Outback, nestled in Star Valley, is the McKinnon family cattle station. Southern Cross Station is an oasis in the harsh Outback landscape and a refuge to the McKinnon family—Kane, Reid and their sister Annie. But it's also full of secrets…

In April don't miss…

THE CATTLEMAN'S ENGLISH ROSE
On sale April 2005 (#3841)

Kane's story. He's keeping a secret, but little does he know that by helping a friend he'll also find a bride!

Coming soon…

THE BLIND DATE SURPRISE
On sale May 2005 (#3845)

It's Annie's turn. How's a young woman supposed to find love when the nearest eligible man lives miles away?

THE MIRRABROOK MARRIAGE
On sale June 2005 (#3849)

And lastly, Reid. He's about to discover a secret that will change his whole life!

HARLEQUIN®
Live the emotion™

www.eHarlequin.com

HRSCR2

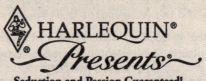

Seduction and Passion Guaranteed!

Introducing a brand-new trilogy by

Sharon Kendrick

Passion, power & privilege — the dynasty continues with these handsome princes...

Welcome to Mardivino—a beautiful and wealthy Mediterranean island principality, with a prestigious and glamorous royal family. There are three Cacciatore princes—Nicolo, Guido and the eldest, the heir, Gianferro.

Next month (May 05), meet Nico in

THE MEDITERRANEAN PRINCE'S PASSION #2466

Coming in June: Guido's story, in

THE PRINCE'S LOVE-CHILD #2472

Coming soon: Gianferro's story in

THE FUTURE KING'S BRIDE

Only from Harlequin Presents

www.eHarlequin.com

HPRHC

Are you getting it at least twice a month?

Here's how: Try RED DRESS INK books on for size & receive two FREE gifts!

Bombshell
by Lynda Curnyn

As Seen on TV
by Sarah Mlynowski

YES! Send my two FREE books.
There's no risk and no purchase required—ever!

Please send me my two FREE tradesize paperback books and bill me just 99¢ for shipping and handling. I may keep the books and return the shipping statement marked "cancel." If I do not cancel, about a month later I will receive 2 additional books at the low price of just $11.00 each in the U.S. or $13.56 each in Canada, a savings of over 15% off the cover price (plus 50¢ shipping and handling per book*). I understand that accepting the two free books places me under no obligation ever to buy any books. I can always return a shipment and cancel at any time. Even if I never buy another book from Red Dress Ink, the free books are mine to keep forever.

160 HDN D367   360 HDN D37K

Name (PLEASE PRINT)

Address   Apt. #

City   State/Prov.   Zip/Postal Code

*Want to try another series? Call 1-800-873-8635
or order online at www.TryRDI.com/free.*

In the U.S. mail to: 3010 Walden Ave., P.O. Box 1867, Buffalo, NY 14240-1867
In Canada mail to: P.O. Box 609, Fort Erie, ON L2A 5X3

*Terms and prices subject to change without notice. Sales tax applicable in N.Y.
**Canadian residents will be charged applicable provincial taxes and GST.
All orders subject to approval. Offer limited to one per household.
® and ™ are trademarks owned by the trademark owner and/or its licensee.

© 2004 Harlequin Enterprises Ltd.

RDI04MMP

eHARLEQUIN.com

The Ultimate Destination for Women's Fiction

Becoming an eHarlequin.com member is easy, fun and **FREE!** Join today to enjoy great benefits:

- **Super savings** on all our books, including members-only discounts and offers!

- Enjoy **exclusive online reads**—FREE!

- Info, tips and **expert advice** on writing your own romance novel.

- FREE romance **newsletters,** customized by you!

- Find out the latest on your **favorite authors.**

- Enter to win exciting **contests and promotions!**

- Chat with other members in our **community message boards!**

To become a member, visit www.eHarlequin.com today!

INTMEMB04R

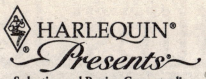

Seduction and Passion Guaranteed!

They're the men who have everything—
except brides...

Wealth, power, charm—what else could a
heart-stoppingly handsome tycoon need?
In the GREEK TYCOONS miniseries you have
already been introduced to some gorgeous Greek
multimillionaires who are in need of wives.

**Now it's the turn of favorite Presents
author Lucy Monroe,
with her attention-grabbing romance**

THE GREEK'S INNOCENT VIRGIN
Coming in May
#2464

www.eHarlequin.com

Be sure to catch your favorite Harlequin Flipside authors writing for other Silhouette and Harlequin series!

SILHOUETTE *Romance*

Holly Jacobs
in Silhouette Romance

ONCE UPON A PRINCESS
May 2005

ONCE UPON A PRINCE
July 2005

ONCE UPON A KING
September 2005

Also watch for:

Stephanie Doyle in Silhouette Bombshell in July 2005

Elizabeth Bevarly, Cindi Myers and Dawn Atkins appearing in Harlequin Blaze in Fall 2005

Stephanie Rowe writing for Harlequin Intrigue in 2006

Barbara Dunlop in Silhouette Desire in 2006

Look for books by these authors at your favorite retail outlet.

www.eHarlequin.com

HFAIOS